INTO THE VOID

A great voice roared out of the night.

"What are you doing there? Come down at once!"

In unreasoning fear, Jefferson Wilkes ran back to the ship. The great hollow shaft only a few feet above his head seemed to offer a second way into the machine—or at least a chance of hiding until he could escape.

He scarcely noticed that the great voice from the night was no longer peremptory, but pleading. He was conscious only of the dark tunnel ahead. Holding his torch in one hand, he began to crawl along it.

When he could go no further, he slumped down. He did not notice, nor could he have understood, the faint wavering glow that was burning in the walls around him.

Suddenly a brilliant light was moving down the tunnel, and behind it was something strange and huge. Then he screamed in terror as metal claws came full into the light and reached forward to grasp him . . .

". . . A SENSITIVE STUDY OF THE MEN BEHIND THE TECHNOLOGIES AND A POETIC AND PHILO-SOPHICAL PROBING OF THE IDEAS AND IDEALS WHICH DRIVE MEN INTO SPACE . . ."

—H. H. Holmes

BOOKS BY ARTHUR C. CLARKE

*Published by Ballantine Books

PRELUDE
TO SPACE

ARTHUR C. CLARKE

BALLANTINE BOOKS • NEW YORK

To my friends in the
British Interplanetary Society—
who by sharing this dream, helped
to make it come true.

Library of Congress Catalog Card Number: 54-7257

ISBN 0-345-25113-X-150

Manufactured in the United States of America

First Ballantine Books Edition: March, 1954
Second Printing: July, 1976

Cover art by Stanislaw Fernandes

Post-Apollo Preface

On July 20, 1969, all the countless science-fiction stories of the first landing on the Moon became frozen in time, like flies in amber. We can look back on them now with a new perspective, and indeed with a new interest—for we know how it was really done, and can judge the accuracy of the predictions.

Now—contrary to a general belief—prediction is *not* the main purpose of science-fiction writers; few, if any, have ever claimed "this is how it will be." Most of them are concerned with the play of ideas, and the exploration of novel concepts in science and discovery. "What if . . . ?" is the thought underlying all writing in this field. What if a man could become invisible? What if we could travel into the future? What if there is intelligent life elsewhere in the Universe? These are the initial grains around which the writer secretes his modest pearl. No one is more surprised than he is, if it turns out that he has indeed forecast the pattern of future events.

Yet it must be admitted that the stories of space travel form an exception to this general rule. Although the earliest works, such as Cyrano de Bergerac's Voyages to the Moon and the Sun, were pure fantasy, most of the tales written in the past hundred years were based as far as possible upon accurate science and foreseeable technology. Their writers did believe that they were predicting the future, at least in general terms. More than that, the pioneers of astronautics used fiction in a deliberate attempt to spread their ideas to the general public. Tsiolkovsky, Oberth, and von Braun all wrote space fiction at one time or another. In so doing, they were not merely predicting the future, they were creating it.

I must confess that I had similar propagandistic ideas in mind when planning this book. It was written in July, 1947, during my summer vacation as a student at King's College, London. The actual composition took exactly twenty days, a record I have never since approached. This speed was largely due to the fact that I had been making notes on the book for more than a year; it was already well organized in my head before I set pen to paper. ("Pen" is correct; the original manuscript was handwritten in a series of school exercise books which were a relic of my Royal Air Force days).

In the twenty-two years between the writing of this book and the actual landing on the Moon, our world has changed almost beyond recognition. The following pages may serve as a useful reminder of the way in which the public attitude toward space travel has also been transformed, particularly in the United States. In 1947, it seemed quite reasonable to base an Interplanetary Project in London; as one of my English characters remarks, "You Americans have always been a bit conservative about space flight, and didn't take it seriously until several years after us." That statement was still true a decade after I had finished the book—when Sputnik I was launched in October, 1957. It is now very hard to realize that right into the late 1950s many American engineers *in the rocket field itself* pooh-poohed the idea of space flight. With a few notable exceptions, the banner of astronautics was borne by Europeans—or former Europeans like Willy Ley, who, alas, died only a few days before Apollo 11 vindicated his dreams of more than forty years.

The modest amounts of money with which I assumed space research could be conducted will now cause some rueful amusement. No one could have imagined, in 1947, that within twenty years not merely millions, but *billions,* of dollars would be budgeted annually for space flight and that a lunar landing would be a primary objective of the two most powerful nations on Earth. Back in the 1940s it seemed most unlikely that governments would put any money into space before private enterprise had shown the way.

I can claim a few successes as a minor prophet. I placed the first lunar impact in 1959, and Luna II hit the Mare Imbrium at 21:01 GMT on September 13, 1959. I was watching hopefully through my Questar telescope in Columbo as the Moon sank into the Indian Ocean, but saw nothing.

Prelude to Space was written just two years after my 1945 paper on synchronous communications satellites and was, therefore, the first work of fiction in which the idea of "comsats" was advocated. I have reason to believe that it had some influence on the men who turned this dream into reality.

The book appeared originally as a paperback (Galaxy Novel No. 3, February 1951) and was thus my first novel to achieve independent publication. The first hard-cover edition appeared in June 1953 (Gnome Press), together with a paperback edition by Ballantine Books. Another publisher, now deservedly extinct, later issued two editions with a change of title, despite my express orders. (For the record, these titles were *Master of Space* and *The Space Dreamers.*) I am now happy to see the return of the Ballantine imprint; the current hard-cover edition is published by Harcourt Brace Jovanovich.

One prediction which gives me much pleasure is that contained in the sentence "Oberth—now an old man of eighty-four—had started the chain reaction which was to lead in his own lifetime to the crossing of space." A reviewer who discussed Oberth's proposals in a leading scientific journal of the 1930s once scoffingly conceded that they might be realized "before the human race became extinct." I am happy to report that Herman Oberth, as a not-so-old man of seventy-five, watched Apollo 11 being launched from Cape Kennedy on July 16, 1969.

While writing this novel, I had the great advantage of access to calculations which my colleagues A.V. Cleaver and L.R. Shepherd (later manager of the Rolls-Royce Rocket Division, and chief executive of the "Dragon" High Temperature Reactor Project) were making on the subject of nuclear rocket propulsion. These were published in their classic paper "The Atomic Rocket," in the Journal of the British Interplanetary Society for September 1948–March 1949, which pioneered this field of studies.

Fifteen years later, atomic rockets of the type they proposed were successfully ground-tested by the A.E.C., and although "Project Rover" was canceled before flights were achieved, some form of nuclear propulsion will be available when we are ready to go to Mars.

In this story I assumed the use of orbital rendezvous techniques, and particularly of reusable boosters which could be flown over and over again. My imagination failed to conceive of multi-million-dollar vehicles like the lunar module and the Saturn-V launcher, which would be discarded after a single mission. But the future of space flight lies with such concepts as those described here; politics, and not economics, has shaped our present systems, and history will soon pass them by. The Space Shuttle will, hopefully, be the first *practical* space transportation vehicle of the 1980s; like my "Beta," it will be winged and fully reusable, capable of making scores of flights.

My little jibe at the late Dr. C.S. Lewis subsequently resulted in an amicable correspondence and a meeting at Oxford's famed Eastgate pub, where

Val Cleaver and I tried to demonstrate to Dr. Lewis (and his companion, Professor J.R.R. Tolkien) that all would-be astronauts were not like the malevolent Weston in *Out of the Silent Planet*. Lewis cheerfully compromised with the observation that though we were probably very wicked people, the world would be an awfully dull place if everyone was good.

Although I am well aware that propaganda is the enemy of art, I am still proud of the fact that this novel's main theme is the absurdity of exporting national rivalries beyond the atmosphere. In 1947, I summed up this concept in the phrase, "We will take no frontiers into space." Exactly twenty years later, the United Nations Space Treaty prohibited territorial claims on any celestial bodies.

That treaty was signed just in time. Only two years later, Neil Armstrong and Edwin Aldrin unveiled the plaque which reads:

> Here men from the planet Earth first
> set foot upon the Moon, July 1969.
> We came in peace for all mankind.

Yet when, in 1947, I set this novel exactly thirty years in the future, I did not *really* believe that a lunar landing would be achieved even by that distant date; I was optimistically whistling in the dark—and perhaps trying to give myself a sixtieth birthday present. I would never have dared to imagine that by 1977 a dozen men would have walked on the Moon, and twenty-seven would have orbited it. Still less could I have imagined that the first nation to reach the Moon would so swiftly abandon it again. . . .

In one sense, the Apollo Project was indeed a Prelude to Space. Now there will be a short interlude; and sometime in the 1980s, the real story will begin.

The hiatus does not disappoint me, for I have already seen achievements beyond my wildest dreams. I have shaken the hands of the first man to orbit the earth, the first man to step out into space, and the first to walk upon the Moon.

In the long perspectives of history, it will not matter that two of them were Russian and one was American.

Arthur C. Clarke,
September 1975

Part One

For five miles straight as an arrow, the gleaming metal track lay along the face of the desert. It pointed to the northwest across the dead heart of the continent and to the ocean beyond. Over this land, once the home of the aborigines, many strange shapes had risen, roaring, in the last generation. The greatest and strangest of them all lay at the head of the launching track along which it was to hurtle into the sky.

A little town had grown out of the desert in this valley between the low hills. It was a town built for one purpose—a purpose which was embodied in the fuel-storage tanks and the power station at the end of the five-mile-long track. Here had gathered scientists and engineers from all the countries of the world. And here the "Prometheus," first of all spaceships, had been assembled in the past three years.

The Prometheus of legend had brought fire from heaven down to earth. The Prometheus of the twentieth century was to take atomic fire back into the home of the Gods, and to prove that Man, by his own exertions, had broken free at last from the chains that held him to his world for a million years.

No one seemed to know who had given the spaceship its name. It was, in actuality, not a single ship at all but really consisted of two separate machines. With

3

notable lack of enterprise, the designers had christened the two components "Alpha" and "Beta." Only the upper component, "Alpha," was a pure rocket. "Beta," to give it its full name, was a "hypersonic athodyd." Most people usually called it an atomic ramjet, which was both simpler and more expressive.

It was a long way from the flying bombs of the Second World War to the two-hundred-ton "Beta," skimming the top of the atmosphere at thousands of miles an hour. Yet both operated on the same principle— the use of forward speed to provide compression for the jet. The main difference lay in the fuel. V.1 had burned gasoline; "Beta" burned plutonium, and her range was virtually unlimited. As long as her air-scoops could collect and compress the tenuous gas of the upper atmosphere, the white-hot furnace of the atomic pile would blast it out of the jets. Only when at last the air was too thin for power or support need she inject into the pile the methane from her fuel tanks and thus become a pure rocket.

"Beta" could leave the atmosphere, but she could never escape completely from Earth. Her task was twofold. First, she had to carry up fuel tanks into the orbit round the Earth, and set them circling like tiny moons until they were needed. Not until this had been done would she lift "Alpha" into space. The smaller ship would then fuel up in free orbit from the waiting tanks, fire its motors to break away from Earth, and make the journey to the Moon.

Circling patiently, "Beta" would wait until the spaceship returned. At the end of its half-million-mile journey "Alpha" would have barely enough fuel to maneuver into a parallel orbit. The crew and their equipment would then be transferred to the waiting "Beta," which would still carry sufficient fuel to bring them safely back to Earth.

It was an elaborate plan, but even with atomic energy it was still the only practicable way of making the lunar round-trip with a rocket weighing not less than many thousands of tons. Moreover, it had many other advantages. "Alpha" and "Beta" could each be designed to carry out their separate tasks with an efficiency which no single, all-purpose ship could hope to achieve. It was impossible to combine in one machine the ability to fly through Earth's atmosphere and to land on the airless Moon.

When the time came to make the next voyage, "Alpha" would still be circling the Earth, to be refuelled in space and used again. No later journey would ever be quite as difficult as the first. In time there would be more efficient motors, and later still, when the lunar colony had been founded, there would be refuelling stations on the Moon. After that it would be easy, and space flight would become a commercial proposition —though this would not happen for half a century or more.

Meanwhile the "Prometheus," alias "Alpha" and "Beta," still lay glistening beneath the Australian sun while the technicians worked over her. The last fittings were being installed and tested: the moment of her destiny was drawing nearer. In a few weeks, if all went well, she would carry the hopes and fears of humanity into the lonely deeps beyond the sky.

1

Dirk Alexson threw down his book and climbed up the short flight of stairs to the observation deck. It was still much too soon to see land, but the journey's approaching end had made him restless and unable to concentrate. He walked over to the narrow, curving windows set in the leading-edge of the great wing and stared down at the featureless ocean below.

There was absolutely nothing to be seen: from this height the Atlantic's mightiest storms would have been invisible. He gazed for a while at the blank grayness beneath and then moved across to the passengers' radar display.

The spinning line of light on the screen had begun to paint the first dim echoes at the limits of its range. Land lay ahead, ten miles below and two hundred miles away—the land that Dirk had never seen though it was sometimes more real to him than the country of his birth. From those hidden shores, over the last four centuries, his ancestors had set out for the New World in search of freedom or fortune. Now he was returning, crossing in less than three hours the wastes over which they had labored for as many weary weeks. And he was coming on a mission of which they, in their wildest imaginings, could never have dreamed.

The luminous image of Land's End had moved halfway across the radar screen before Dirk first glimpsed the advancing coastline, a dark stain almost lost in the horizon mists. Though he had sensed no change of direction, he knew that the liner must now be falling down the long slope that led to London Airport, four hundred miles away. In a few minutes he would hear again, faint but infinitely reassuring, the rumbling whisper of the great jets as the air thickened around him and brought their music once more to his ears.

Cromwall was a gray blur, sinking astern too swiftly for any details to be seen. For all that one could tell, King Mark might still be waiting above the cruel rocks for the ship that brought Iseult, while on the hills Merlin might yet be talking with the winds and thinking of his doom. From this height the land would have looked the same when the masons laid the last stone on Tintagel's walls.

Now the liner was dropping toward a cloudscape so white and dazzling that it hurt the eyes. At first it seemed broken only by a few slight undulations but, presently, as it rose toward him, Dirk realized that the mountains of cloud below were built on a Himalayan scale. A moment later, the peaks were above him and the machine was driving through a great pass flanked on either side by overhanging walls of snow. He flinched involuntarily as the white cliffs came racing toward him, then relaxed as the driving mist was all around and he could see no more.

The cloud layer must have been very thick, for he caught only the briefest glimpse of London and was taken almost unaware by the gentle shock of landing. Then the sounds of the outer world came rushing in upon his mind—the metallic voices of loud-speakers, the clanging of hatches, and above all these, the dying fall of the great turbines as they idled to rest.

The wet concrete, the waiting trucks, and the gray clouds lowering overhead dispelled the last impressions of romance or adventure. It was drizzling slightly, and as the ridiculously tiny tractor hauled the great ship away, her glistening sides made her seem a creature of the deep sea rather than of the open sky. Above the jet housings, little flurries of steam were rising as the water drained down the wing.

Much to his relief, Dirk was met at the Customs barrier. As his name was checked off the passenger list, a stout, middle-aged man came forward with outstretched hand.

"Dr. Alexson? Pleased to meet you. My name's Matthews. I'm taking you to Headquarters at Southbank and generally looking after you while you're in London."

"Glad to hear it," smiled Dirk. "I suppose I can thank McAndrews for this?"

"That's right. I'm his assistant in Public Relations. Here—let me have that bag. We're going by the express tube; it's the quickest way—and the best, since you get into the city without having to endure the suburbs. There's one snag, though."

"What's that?"

Matthews sighed. "You'd be surprised at the number of visitors who cross the Atlantic safely, then disappear into the Underground and are never seen again."

Matthews never even smiled as he imparted this unlikely news. As Dirk was to discover, his impish sense of humor seemed to go with a complete incapacity for laughter. It was a most disconcerting combination.

"There's one thing I'm not at all clear about," began Matthews as the long red train began to draw out of the airport station. "We get a lot of American scientists over to see us, but I understand that science isn't your line."

"No, I'm an historian."

Matthews's eyebrows asked an almost audible question.

"I suppose it must be rather puzzling," continued Dirk, "but it's quite logical. In the past, when history was made, there was seldom anyone around to record it properly. Nowadays, of course, we have newspapers and films—but it's surprising what important features get overlooked simply because everyone takes them for granted at the time. Well, the project you people are working on is one of the biggest in history, and if it comes off it will change the future as perhaps no other single event has ever done. So my University decided that there should be a professional historian around to fill in the gaps that might be overlooked."

Matthews nodded.

"Yes, that's reasonable enough. It will make a pleasant change for us non-scientific people, too. We're rather tired of conversations in which three words out of four are mathematical symbols. Still, I suppose you have a fairly good technical background?"

Dirk looked slightly uncomfortable.

"To tell the truth," he confessed, "it's almost fifteen years since I did any science—and I never took it very seriously then. I'll have to learn what I need as I go along."

"Don't worry; we have a high-pressure course for tired businessmen and perplexed politicians which will give you everything you need. And you'll be surprised to find how much you pick up, simply by listening to the Boffins holding forth."

"Boffins?"

"Good lord, don't you know *that* word? It goes back

to the War, and means any long-haired scientific type with a slide-rule in his vest-pocket. I'd better warn you right away that we've quite a private vocabulary here which you'll have to learn. There are so many new ideas and conceptions in our work that we've had to invent new words. You should have brought along a philologist as well!"

Dirk was silent. There were moments when the sheer immensity of his task almost overwhelmed him. Some time in the next six months the work of thousands of men over half a century would reach its culmination. It would be his duty, and his privilege, to be present while history was being made out there in the Australian desert on the other side of the world. He must look upon these events through the eyes of the future, and must record them so that in centuries to come other men could recapture the spirit of this age and time.

They emerged at New Waterloo station, and walked the few hundred yards to the Thames. Matthews had been right in saying that this was the best way to meet London for the first time. The spacious sweep of the fine new Embankment, still only twenty years old, carried Dirk's gaze down the river until it was caught and held by the dome of St. Paul's, glistening wetly in an unexpected shaft of sunlight. He followed the river upstream, past the great white buildings before Charing Cross, but the Houses of Parliament were invisible around the curve of the Thames.

"Quite a view, isn't it?" said Matthews presently. "We're rather proud of it now, but thirty years ago this part was a horrid mass of wharves and mudbanks. By the way—you see that ship over there?"

"You mean the one tied up against the other bank?"

"Yes, do you know what it is?"

"I've no idea."

"She's the *Discovery*, which took Captain Scott into the Antarctic back at the beginning of this century. I often look at her as I come to work and wonder what he'd have thought of the little trip *we* are planning."

Dirk stared intently at the graceful wooden hull, the slim masts and the battered smokestack. His mind slipped into the past in the easy way it had, and it seemed that the Embankment was gone and that the old ship was steaming past walls of ice into an unknown land. He could understand Matthew's feelings, and the sense of historical continuity was suddenly very strong. The line that stretched through Scott back to Drake and Raleigh and yet earlier voyages was still unbroken: only the scale of things had changed.

"Here we are," said Matthews in a tone of proud apology. "It's not as impressive as it might be, but we didn't have a lot of money when we built it. Not that we have now, for that matter."

The white, three-story building that faced the river was unpretentious and had obviously been constructed only a few years before. It was surrounded by large, open lawns scantily covered by dispirited grass. Dirk guessed that they had already been earmarked for future building operations. The grass seemed to have realized this too.

Nevertheless, as administrative buildings went, Headquarters was not unattractive, and the view over the river was certainly very fine. Along the second story ran a line of letters, as clean-cut and severely practical as the rest of the buildings. They formed a single word, but at the sight of it Dirk felt a curious tingling in his veins. It seemed out of place, somehow, here in the heart of a great city where millions were concerned with the affairs of everyday life. It was as out of place as the *Discovery,* lying against the far bank at the end of her long journeying—and it spoke of a longer voyage than she or any ship had ever made:

INTERPLANETARY

2

The office was small, and he would have to share it with a couple of junior draftsmen—but it overlooked the Thames and when he was tired of his reports and files Dirk could always rest his eyes on that great dome floating above Ludgate Hill. From time to time Matthews or his chief would drop in for a talk, but usually they left him alone, knowing that that was his desire. He was anxious to be left in peace until he had burrowed through the hundreds of reports and books which Matthews had obtained for him.

It was a far cry from Renaissance Italy to twentieth-century London, but the techniques he had acquired when writing his thesis on Lorenzo the Magnificent served Dirk in good stead now. He could tell, almost at a glance, what was unimportant and what must be studied carefully. In a few days the outlines of the story were complete and he could begin to fill in the details.

The dream was older than he had imagined. Two thousand years ago the Greeks had guessed that the Moon was a world not unlike the Earth, and in the second century A.D. the satirist Lucian had written the first of all interplanetary romances. It had taken more than seventeen centuries to bridge the gulf between fiction and reality—and almost all the progress had been made in the last fifty years.

The modern era had begun in 1923, when an obscure Transylvanian professor named Hermann Oberth had published a pamphlet entitled *The Rocket Into Interplanetary Space*. In this he developed for the first time the mathematics of space flight. Leafing through the pages of one of the few copies still in existence, Dirk found it hard to believe that so enormous a superstructure had arisen from so small a beginning. Oberth—now an old man of 84—had started

11

the chain reaction which was to lead in his own life-time to the crossing of space.

In the decade before the Second World War, Oberth's German disciples had perfected the liquid-fuelled rocket. At first they too had dreamed of the conquest of space, but that dream had been forgotten with the coming of Hitler. The city over which Dirk so often gazed still bore the scars from the time, thirty years ago, when the great rockets had come falling down from the stratosphere in a tumult of sundered air.

Less than a year later had come that dreary dawn in the New Mexico desert, when it seemed that the River of Time had halted for a moment, then plunged in foam and spray into a new channel toward a changed and unknown future. With Hiroshima had come the end of a war and the end of an age: the power and the machine had come together at last and the road to space lay clear ahead.

It had been a steep road, and it had taken thirty years to climb—thirty years of triumphs and heart-breaking disappointments. As he grew to know the men around him, as he listened to their stories and their conversations, Dirk slowly filled in the personal details which the reports and summaries could never provide.

"The television picture wasn't too clear, but every few seconds it steadied and we got a good image. That was the biggest thrill of my life—being the first man to see the other side of the Moon. Going there will be a bit of an anti-climax."

"—most terrific explosion you ever saw. When we got up, I heard Goering say: 'If *that's* the best you can do, I'll tell the Fuehrer the whole thing's a waste of money.' You should have seen von Braun's face——"

"The KX 14's still up there: she completes one or-bit every three hours, which was just what we'd in-tended. But the blasted radio transmitter failed at take-off, so we never got those instrument readings after all."

"I was looking through the twelve-inch reflector when that load of magnesium powder hit the Moon, about fifty kilometers from Aristarchus. You can just see the crater it made, if you have a look around sunset."

Sometimes Dirk envied these men. They had a purpose in life, even if it was one he could not fully understand. It must give them a feeling of power to send their great machines thousands of miles out into space. But power was dangerous, and often corrupting. Could they be trusted with the forces they were bringing into the world? Could the world itself be trusted with them?

Despite his intellectual background, Dirk was not altogether free from the fear of science that had been common ever since the great discoveries of the Victorian era. He felt not only isolated but sometimes a little nervous in his new surroundings. The few people he spoke to were invariably helpful and polite, but a certain shyness and his anxiety to master the background of his subject in the shortest time kept him away from all social entanglements. He liked the atmosphere of organization, which was almost aggressively democratic, and later on it would be easy enough to meet all the people he wished.

At the moment, Dirk's chief contacts with anyone outside the Public Relations Department were at mealtimes. Interplanetary's small canteen was patronized, in relays, by all the staff from the Director General downwards. It was run by a very enterprising committee with a fondness for experimenting, and although there were occasional culinary catastrophes, the food was usually very good. For all that Dirk could tell, Interplanetary's boast of the best cooking on Southbank might indeed be justified.

As Dirk's lunch-time, like Easter, was a movable feast, he usually met a fresh set of faces every day and soon grew to know most of the important members of the organization by sight. No one took any notice of him: the building was full of birds-of-passage from universities and industrial firms all over the world, and he was obviously regarded as just another visiting scientist.

His college, through the ramifications of the United States Embassy, had managed to find Dirk a small service flat a few hundred yards from Grosvenor Square. Every morning he walked to Bond Street Station and took the Tube to Waterloo. He quickly learned to avoid the early-morning rush, but he was seldom much later than many senior members of Interplanetary's staff. Eccentric hours were popular at Southbank: though Dirk sometimes remained in the building until midnight, there were always sounds of activity around him—usually from the research sections. Often, in order to clear his head and get a little exercise, he would go for a stroll along the deserted corridors, making mental notes of interesting departments which he might one day visit officially. He learned a great deal more about the place in this way than from the elaborate and much-amended organization charts which Matthews had lent him—and was always borrowing back again.

Frequently Dirk would come across half-opened doors revealing vistas of untidy labs and machine-shops in which gloomy technicians sat gazing at equipment which was obviously refusing to behave. If the hour was very late, the scene would be softened by a mist of tobacco-smoke and invariably an electric kettle and a battered tea pot would occupy places of honor in the near foreground. Occasionally Dirk would arrive at some moment of technical triumph, and if he was not careful he was likely to be invited to share the ambiguous liquid which the engineers were continually brewing. In this way he became on nodding terms with a great many people, but he knew scarcely a dozen well enough to address them by name.

At the age of thirty-three, Dirk Alexson was still somewhat nervous of the everyday world around him.

He was happier in the past and among his books, and though he had traveled fairly extensively in the United States, he had spent almost all his life in academic circles. His colleagues recognized him as a steady, sound worker with an almost intuitive flair for unraveling complicated situations. No one knew if he would make a great historian, but his study of the Medicis had been acknowledged as outstanding. His friends had never been able to understand how anyone of Dirk's somewhat placid disposition could so accurately have analyzed the motives and behavior of that flamboyant family.

Pure chance, it seemed, had brought him from Chicago to London, and he was still very much conscious of the fact. A few months ago the influence of Walter Pater had begun to wane: the little, crowded stage of Renaissance Italy was losing its charm—if so mild a word could be applied to that microcosm of intrigues and assassinations. It had not been his first change of interest, and he feared it would not be his last, for Dirk Alexson was still seeking a work to which he could devote his life. In a moment of depression he had remarked to his Dean that probably only the future held a subject which would really appeal to him. That casual and half-serious complaint had coincided with a letter from the Rockefeller Foundation, and before he knew it Dirk had been on the way to London.

For the first few days he was haunted by the spector of his own incapacity, but he had learned now that this always happened when he started a new job and it had ceased to be more than a nuisance. After about a week he felt that he now had a fairly clear picture of the organization in which he had so unexpectedly found himself. His confidence began to return, and he could relax a little.

Since undergraduate days he had kept a desultory journal—usually neglected save in occasional crises—and he now began once more to record his impressions and the everyday events of his life. These notes, written for his own satisfaction, would enable him to marshal his thoughts and might later serve as a basis for the official history he must one day produce.

"Today, May 3, 1978, I've been in London for exactly a week—and I've seen nothing of it except the areas around Bond Street and Waterloo. When it's fine Matthews and I usually go for a stroll along the river after lunch. We go across the "New" bridge (which has only been built for about forty years!) and walk up or down river as the fancy takes us, crossing again at Charing Cross or Blackfriars. There are quite a number of variations, clockwise and counter-clockwise.

"Alfred Matthews is about forty, and I've found him very helpful. He has an extraordinary sense of humor, but I've never seen him smile—he's absolutely deadpan. He seems to know his job pretty well—a good deal better, I should say, than McAndrews, who is supposed to be his boss. Mac is about ten years older: like Alfred, he graduated through journalism into public relations. He's a lean, hungry-looking person and usually speaks with a slight Scots accent—which vanishes completely when he's excited. This should prove something, but I can't imagine what. He's not a bad fellow, but I don't think he's very bright. Alfred does all the work and there's not much love lost between them. It's sometimes a bit difficult keeping on good terms with them both.

"Next week I hope to start meeting people and going further afield. I particularly want to meet the crew —but I'm keeping out of the scientists' way until I know a bit more about atomic drives and interplanetary orbits. Alfred is going to teach me all about this next week—so he says. What I also hope to discover is how such an extraordinary hybrid as Interplanetary was ever formed in the first place. It seems a typically British compromise, and there's very little on paper about its formation and origins. The whole institution is a mass of paradoxes. It exists in a state of chronic bankruptcy, yet it's responsible for spending something like ten millions a year (£, not $). The Government has very little in its administration, and in some ways it seems as autocratic as the B.B.C. But when it's attacked in Parliament (which happens every other month) some Minister always gets up to defend it. Perhaps, after all, Mac's a better organizer than I imagine!

"I called it 'British,' but of course it isn't. About a fifth of the staff are American, and I've heard every conceivable accent in the canteen. It's as international as the United Nations secretariat, though the British certainly provide most of the driving force and the administrative staff. Why this should be, I don't know: perhaps Matthews can explain.

"Another query: apart from their accents, it's very difficult to see any real distinction between the different nationalities here. Is this due to the—to put it mildly—supranational nature of their work? And if I stay here long enough, I suppose I shall get deracinated too."

3

"I was wondering," said McAndrews, "when you were going to ask that question. The answer's rather complicated."

"I'll be very much surprised," Dirk answered dryly, "if it's quite as involved as the machinations of the Medici family."

"Perhaps not; we've never used assassination yet, though we've often felt like it. Miss Reynolds, will you take any calls while I talk with Dr. Alexson? Thank you.

"Well, as you know, the foundations of astronautics —the science of space travel—had been pretty well laid at the end of the Second World War. V. 2 and atomic energy had convinced most people that space could be crossed, if anyone wanted to do it. There were several societies, in England and the States, actively promulgating the idea that we should go to the

Moon and the planets. They made steady but slow progress until the 1950's, when things really started to get moving.

"In 1959, as you may—er—just remember, the American Army's guided missile 'Orphan Annie' hit the Moon with twenty-five pounds of flash-powder aboard. From that moment, the public began to realize that space travel wasn't a thing of the distant future, but might come inside a generation. Astronomy began to replace atomic physics as the Number One science, and the rocket societies' membership lists started to lengthen steadily. But it was one thing to crash an un-manned projectile into the Moon—and quite another to land a full-sized spaceship there and bring it home again. Some pessimists thought the job might still take another hundred years.

"There were a lot of people in this country who didn't intend to wait that long. They believed that the crossing of space was as essential for progress as the discovery of the New World had been four hundred years before. It would open up new frontiers and give the human race a goal so challenging that it would overshadow national differences and put the tribal con-flicts of the early twentieth century in their true per-spective. Energies that might have gone into wars would be fully employed in the colonization of the planets—which could certainly keep us busy for a good many centuries. That was the theory, at any rate.

McAndrews smiled a little.

"There were, of course, a good many other motives. You know what an unsettled period the early 50's was. The cynic's argument for space flight was summed up in the famous remark: 'Atomic power makes inter-planetary travel not only possible but imperative.' As long as it was confined to Earth, humanity had too many eggs in one rather fragile basket.

"All this was realized by an oddly assorted group of scientists, writers, astonomers, editors, and buiness-men in the old Interplanetary Society. With very small capital, they started the publication *Spacewards,* which was inspired by the success of the American National Geographic Society's magazine. What the N.G.S. had done for the Earth could, it was argued, now be done for the solar system. *Spacewards* was an attempt to make the public shareholders, as it were, in the conquest of space. It catered to the new interest in astronomy, and those who subscribed to it felt that they were helping to finance the first space flight.

"The project wouldn't have succeeded a few years earlier, but the time was now ripe for it. In a few years there were about a quarter of a million subscribers all over the world, and in 1962 'Interplanetary' was founded to carry out full-time research into the problems of space flight. At first it couldn't offer the salaries of the great government-sponsored rocket establishments, but slowly it attracted the best scientists in the field. They preferred working on a constructive project, even at lower pay, to building missiles for transporting atomic bombs. In the early days, the organization was also helped by one or two financial windfalls. When the last British millionaire died in 1965, he balked the Treasury of almost all his fortune by making it into a Trust Fund for our use.

"From the first, Interplanetary was a world-wide organization and it's largely an historical accident that its H.Q. is actually in London. It might very well have been in America, and a lot of our compatriots are still annoyed that it isn't. But for some reason, you Americans have always been a bit conservative about space flight, and didn't take it seriously until several years after us. Never mind: the Germans beat us both.

"Also, you must remember that the United States is much too small a country for astronautical research. Yes, I know that sounds odd—but if you look at a population map you'll see what I mean. There are only two places in the world that are really suitable for long-range rocket research. One's the Sahara desert, and even that is a little too near the great cities of Europe. The other is the West Australian desert, where the British Government started building its great rocket range in 1947. It's more than a thousand miles long, and there's another two thousand miles of ocean beyond it—giving a grand total of over three thousand miles. You won't find any place in the United States where you can safely fire a rocket even five hundred miles. So it's partly a geographical accident that things have turned out this way.

"Where was I? Oh yes, up to 1960 or so. It was about then that we began to get really important, for two reasons which aren't widely known. By that time a whole section of nuclear physics had come to a full stop. The scientists of the Atomic Development Authority thought they could start the hydrogen-helium reaction—and I don't mean the tritium reaction of the old H-bomb—but the crucial experiments had been very wisely banned. There's rather a lot of hydrogen in the sea! So the nuclear physicists were all sitting around chewing their fingernails until we could build them laboratories out in space. It wouldn't matter, then, if something went wrong. The solar system would merely acquire a second and rather temporary sun. ADA also wanted us to dump the dangerous fission products from the piles, which were too radioactive to keep on Earth but which might be useful some day.

"The second reason wasn't so spectacular, but was perhaps even more immediately important. The great radio and telegraph companies *had* to get out into space—it was the only way they could broadcast television over the whole world and provide a universal communication service. As you know, the very short waves of radar and television won't bend around the Earth—they travel in practically straight lines, so that one station can send signals only as far as the horizon. Airborne relays had been built to get over this difficulty, but it was realized that the final solution would be reached only when repeater stations could be built thousands of miles above the Earth—artificial moons, probably traveling in twenty-four-hour orbits so that they'd appear stationary in the sky. No doubt you've read all about these ideas, so I won't go into them now.

"So by about 1970 we had the support of some of the world's biggest technical organizations, with virtually unlimited funds. They *had* to come to us, since we had all the experts. In the early days, I'm afraid there was a certain amount of bickering and the Service Departments have never quite forgiven us for stealing back all their best scientists. But on the whole we get along well enough with ADA, Westinghouse, General Electric, Rolls-Royce, Lockheeds, de Havillands, and the rest of them. They've all got offices here, as you've probably noticed. Although they make us very substantial grants, the technical services they provide are really beyond price. Without their help, I don't suppose we'd have reached this stage for another twenty years."

There was a brief pause, and Dirk emerged from the torrent of words like a spaniel clambering out of a mountain stream. McAndrews talked much too quickly, obviously repeating phrases and whole paragraphs which he had been using for years. Dirk got the impression that almost everything he had said had probably come from other sources, and wasn't original at all.

"I'd no idea," he replied, "just how extensive your ramifications were."

"Believe me, that's nothing!" McAndrews exclaimed. "I don't think there are many big industrial firms who haven't been convinced that we can help them in some way. The cable companies will save hundreds of millions when they can replace their ground stations and land-lines by a few repeaters in space; the chemical industry will——"

"Oh, I'll take your word for it! I was wondering where all the money came from, and now I see just how big a thing this is."

"Don't forget," interjected Matthews, who had hitherto been sitting in resigned silence, "our most important contribution to industry."

"What's that?"

"The import of high-grade vacuums for filling electric-light bulbs and electronics tubes."

"Ignoring Alfred's usual facetiousness," said McAndrews severely, "it's perfectly true that physics in general will make tremendous strides when we can build laboratories in space. And you can guess how the astronomers are looking forward to observatories which will never be bothered by clouds."

"I know now," said Dirk, ticking off the points on his fingers, "just *how* Interplanetary happened, and also what it hopes to do. But I still find it very hard to define exactly what it *is*."

"Legally, it's a non-profit-making ("And how!" interjected Matthews, *sotto voce*) organization devoted, as its charter says, 'to research into the problems of space flight.' It orginally obtained its funds from *Spacewards,* but that hasn't any official connection with us now that it's linked up with *National Geographic*—thought it has plenty of unofficial ones. Today most of our money comes from government grants and from industrial concerns. When interplanetary travel is fully established on a commercial basis, as aviation is today, we'll probably evolve into something different. There are a lot of political angles to the whole thing and no one can say just what will happen when the planets start to be colonized."

McAndrews gave a little laugh, half apologetic and half defensive.

"There are a lot of pipe-dreams floating around this place, as you'll probably discover. Some people have ideas of starting scientific utopias on suitable worlds, and all that sort of thing. But the immediate aim is purely technical: we must find out what the planets are like before we decide how to use them."

The office became quiet; for a moment no one seemed inclined to speak. For the first time Dirk realized the true importance of the goal toward which these men were working. He felt overwhelmed and more than a little frightened. Was humanity ready to be pitchforked out into space, ready to face the challenge of barren and inhospitable worlds never meant for Man? He could not be sure, and in the depths of his mind he felt profoundly disturbed.

4

From the street, 53 Rochdale Avenue, S.W.5, appeared to be one of those neo-Georgian residences which the more successful stockbrokers of the early twentieth century had erected as shelters for their declining years. It was set well back from the road, with tastefully laid out but somewhat neglected lawns and flower beds. When the weather was fine, as it occasionally was in the spring of 1978, five young men might sometimes be seen performing desultory gardening operations with inadequate tools. It was clear that they were doing this merely as a relaxation, and that their minds were very far away. Just how far, a casual passer-by could hardly have guessed.

It had been a very well kept secret, largely because the security organizers themselves were ex-newspapermen. As far as the world knew, the crew of the "Prometheus" had not been chosen, whereas in actuality its training had begun more than a year ago. It had continued with quiet efficiency, not five miles from Fleet Street, yet altogether free from the fierce limelight of public interest.

At any time, there were not likely to be more than a handful of men in the world who would be capable of piloting a spaceship. No other work had ever demanded such a unique combination of physical and mental characteristics. The perfect pilot had not only to be a first-class astronomer, an expert engineer and a specialist in electronics, but must be capable of operating efficiently both when he was "weightless" and when the rocket's acceleration made him weigh a quarter of a ton.

No single individual could meet these requirements, and many years ago it had been decided that the crew of a spaceship must consist of at least three men, any two of whom could take over the duties of a third in an emergency. Interplanetary was training five; two were reserves in case of last-minute illness. As yet, no one knew who the two reserves would be.

Few doubted that Victor Hassell would be the ship's captain. At twenty-eight, he was the only man in the world who had logged over a hundred hours in free fall. The record had been entirely accidental. Two years before, Hassell had taken an experimental rocket up into an orbit and circled the world thirty times before he could repair a fault which had developed in the firing circuits, and so reduce his velocity enough to fall back to Earth. His nearest rival, Pierre Leduc, had a mere twenty hours of oribital flight to his credit.

The three remaining men were not professional pilots at all. Arnold Clinton, the Australian, was an electronic engineer and a specialist in computers and automatic controls. Astronomy was represented by the brilliant young American Lewis Taine, whose prolonged absence from Mount Palomar Observatory was now requiring elaborate explanations. The Atomic Development Authority had contributed James Richards, expert on nuclear propulsion systems. Being a ripe old thirty-five, he was usually called "Grandpop" by his colleagues.

Life at the "Nursery," as it was always referred to by those sharing the secret, combined the characteristics of college, monastery and operational bomber station. It was colored by the personalities of the five "pupils," and by the visiting scientists who came in an endless stream to impart their knowledge or, sometimes, to get it back with interest. It was an intensely busy but a happy life, for it had a purpose and a goal.

There was only one shadow, and that was inevitable. When the time for the decision came, no one knew who was to be left behind on the desert sands, watching the "Prometheus" shrink into the sky until the thunder of its jets could be heard no more.

An astrogation lecture was in full swing when Dirk and Matthews tiptoed into the back of the room. The speaker gave them an unfriendly look, but the five men seated around him never even glanced at the intruders. As unobtrusively as possible, Dirk studied them while his guide indicated their names in hoarse whispers.

Hassell he recognized from newspaper photographs, but the others were unknown to him. Rather to Dirk's surprise, they conformed to no particular type. Their only obvious points in common were age, intelligence, and alertness. From time to time they shot questions at the lecturer, and Dirk gathered that they were discussing the landing maneuvers on the Moon. All the conversation was so much above his head that he quickly grew tired of listening and was glad when Matthews gave an interrogatory nod toward the door.

Out in the corridor, they relaxed and lit cigarettes.

"Well," said Matthews, "now that you've seen our guinea pigs, what do you think of them?"

"I can hardly judge. What I'd like to do is meet them informally and just talk with them by themselves."

Matthews blew a smoke-ring and watched it thoughtfully as it dispersed.

"That wouldn't be easy. As you can guess, they haven't much spare time. When they've finished here, they usually disappear in a cloud of dust back to their families."

"How many of them are married?"

"Leduc's got two children; so has Richards. Vic Hassell was married about a year ago. The others are still single."

Dirk wondered what the wives thought about the

whole business. Somehow it didn't seem altogether fair to them. He wondered, too, whether the men regarded this as simply another job of work, or if they felt the exaltation—there was no other word for it —which had obviously inspired the founders of Interplanetary.

They had now come to a door labeled "KEEP OUT—TECHNICAL STAFF ONLY!" Matthews pushed tentatively against it and it swung open.

"Careless!" he said. "There doesn't seem to be anyone around, either. Let's go in—I think this is one of the most interesting places I know, even though I'm not a scientist."

That was one of Matthews' favorite phrases, which probably concealed a well-buried inferiority complex. Actually both he and McAndrews knew far more about science than they pretended.

Dirk followed him into the semi-gloom, then gasped with amazement as Matthews found the switch and the place was flooded with light. He was standing in a control room, surrounded by banks of switches and meters. The only furniture consisted of three luxurious seats suspended in a complex gimbal system. He reached out to touch one of them and it began to rock gently to and fro.

"Don't touch anything," warned Matthews quickly. "We're not really supposed to be in here, in case you hadn't noticed."

Dirk examined the array of controls and switches from a respectful distance. He could guess the purpose of some from the labels they bore, but others were quite incomprehensible. The words "Manual" and "Auto" occurred over and over again. Almost as popular were "Fuel," "Drive Temperature," "Pressure," and "Earth Range." Others, such as "Emergency Cut-out," "Air Warning," and "Pile Jettison" had a distinctly ominous flavor. A third and still more enigmatic group provided grounds for endless speculation. "Alt. Trig. Sync.," "Neut. Count," and "Video

Mix" were perhaps the choicest specimens in this category.

"You'd almost think, wouldn't you," said Matthews, "that the house was ready to take off at any moment. It's a complete mock-up, of course, of 'Alpha's' control room. I've seen them training on it, and it's fascinating to watch even if you don't quite know what it's all about."

Dirk gave a somewhat forced laugh.

"It's a bit eerie, coming across a spaceship control panel in a quiet London suburb."

"It won't be quiet next week. We're throwing it open to the Press then, and we'll probably be lynched for keeping all this under cover so long."

"Next week?"

"Yes, if everything goes according to plan. 'Beta' should have passed her final full-speed tests by then, and we'll all be packing our trunks for Australia. By the way, have you seen those films of the first launchings?"

"No."

"Remind me to let you see them—they're most impressive."

"What's she done so far?"

"Four and a half miles a second with full load. That's a bit short of orbital speed, but everything was still working perfectly. It's a pity, though, that we can't test 'Alpha' before the actual flight."

"When will that be?"

"It's not fixed yet, but we know that the take-off will be when the Moon's entering her first quarter. The ship will land in the Mare Imbrium region while it's still early morning. The return's scheduled for the late afternoon, so they'll have about ten Earth-days there."

"Why the Mare Imbrium, in particular?"

"Because it's flat, very well mapped, and has some of the most interesting scenery on the Moon. Besides, spaceships have *always* landed there since Jules Verne's time. I guess that you know that the name means 'Sea of Rains.'"

"I did know Latin pretty thoroughly once upon a time," Dirk said dryly.

Matthews came as near a smile as he had ever known him to.

"I suppose you did. But let's get out of here before we're caught. Seen enough?"

"Yes, thanks. It's a bit overwhelming, but not so very much worse than a transcontinental jet's cockpit."

"It is if you know what goes on behind all those panels," said Matthews grimly. "Arnold Clinton—that's the electronics king—once told me that there are three thousand tubes in the computing and control circuits alone. And there must be a good many hundreds on the communications side."

Dirk scarcely heard him. He was beginning to realize, for the first time, how swiftly the sands were running out. When he had arrived a fortnight ago, the take-off still seemed a remote event in the indefinite future. That was the general impression in the outside world; now it seemed completely false. He turned to Matthews in genuine bewilderment.

"Your Public Relations Department," he complained, "seems to have misled everyone pretty efficiently. What's the idea?"

"It's purely a matter of policy," replied the other. "In the old days we had to talk big and make spectacular promises to attract any attention at all. Now we prefer to say as little as possible until everything's cut and dried. It's the only way to avoid fantastic rumors and the resulting sense of anticlimax. Do you remember the KY 15? She was the first manned ship to reach an altitude of a thousand miles—but months before she was ready everyone thought that we were going to send her to the Moon. They were disappointed, of course, when she did exactly what she'd been designed for. So nowadays I sometimes call my office the 'Department of Negative Publicity.' It will be quite a relief when the whole thing's over and we can go into forward gear again."

This, thought Dirk, was a very self-centered outlook. It seemed to him that the five men he had just been watching had far better reasons for wishing that the "whole thing was over."

5

"So far," wrote Dirk in his Journal that night, "I've only nibbled round the edges of Interplanetary. Matthews has kept me orbiting around him like a minor planet—I must reach parabolic velocity and escape elsewhere. (I'm beginning to pick up the language, as he promised!)

"The people I want to meet now are the scientists and engineers who are the real driving force behind the organization. What makes them tick, to put it crudely? Are they a lot of Frankensteins merely interested in a technical project without any regard for its consequences? Or do they see, perhaps more clearly than McAndrews and Matthews, just where all this is going to lead? M. and M. sometimes remind me of a couple of real-estate agents trying to sell the Moon. They're doing a job, and doing it well—but someone must have inspired them in the first place. And in any case, they are a grade or two from the top of the hierarchy.

"The Director-General seemed a very interesting personality when I met him for those few minutes the day I arrived—but I can hardly go and catechize *him!* The Deputy D.-G. might have been a good bet, since we're both Californians, but he's not back from the States.

"Tomorrow I get the 'Astronautics Without Tears' course that Matthews promised me when I came. Apparently it's a six-reel instructional film, and I've not been able to see it before because no one in this hotbed of genius was able to repair a thirty-five-millimeter projector. When I've sat through it, Alfred swears I'll be able to hold my own with the astronomers.

"As a good historian, I suppose I should have no prejudices one way or the other, but should be capable of watching Interplanetary's activities with a dispassionate eye. It isn't working out that way. I'm beginning to worry more and more about the ultimate consequences of this work, and the platitudes that Alfred and Mac keep bringing up don't satisfy me at all. I suppose that's why I'm now anxious to get hold of the top scientists and hear their views. Then, perhaps, I'll be able to pass judgment—if it's my job to pass judgment.

"*Later.* Of course it's my job. Look at Gibbon, look at Toynbee. Unless an historian draws conclusions (right or wrong) he's merely a file clerk.

"*Later Still.* How could I have forgotten? Tonight I came up to Oxford Circus in one of the new turbine buses. It's very quiet, but if you listen carefully you can hear it singing to itself in a faint, extremely high soprano. The Londoners are excessively proud of them, since they're the first in the world. I don't understand why a simple thing like a bus should have taken almost as long to develop as a spaceship, but they tell me it has. Something to do with engineering economics, I believe.

"I decided to walk to the flat, and coming out of Bond Street I saw a gilded, horse-drawn van looking as if it had rolled straight out of *Pickwick*. It was delivering goods for some tailor, I believe, and the ornamental lettering said: 'Est. 1768.'

"This sort of thing makes the British very disconcerting people to a foreigner. Of course, McAndrews would say that it's the English, not the British, who are crazy —but I refuse to draw this rather fine distinction."

6

"You'll excuse me for leaving you," said Matthews apologetically, "but although it's a very good film, I'd scream the place down if I had to see it again. At a guess, I've sat through it at least fifty times already."

"That's O.K.," laughed Dirk, from the depths of his seat in the little auditorium. "It's the first time I've ever been the only customer at a movie, so it will be a novel experience."

"Right. I'll be back when it's finished. If you want any reels run through again, just tell the operator."

Dirk settled back into the seat. It was, he reflected, just not comfortable enough to encourage one to relax and take life easily. Which showed good sense on the part of the designer, since this cinema was a strictly functional establishment.

The title with a few brief credits flashed on the screen.

THE ROAD TO SPACE
Technical advice and special effects by Interplanetary.
Produced by Eagle-Lion.

The screen was dark: then, in its center, a narrow band of starlight appeared. It slowly widened, and Dirk realized that he was beneath the opening hemispheres of some great observatory dome. The star-field commenced to expand: he was moving toward it.

"For two thousand years," said a quiet voice, "men have dreamed of journeys to other worlds. The stories of interplanetary flight are legion, but not until our own age was the machine perfected which could make these dreams come true."

Something dark was silhouetted against the star-field—something slim and pointed and eager to be away. The scene lightened and the stars vanished.

31

Only the great rocket remained, its silver hull glistening in the sunlight as it rested upon the desert.

The sands seemed to boil as the blast ate into them. Then the giant projectile was climbing steadily, as if along an invisible wire. The camera tilted upward: the rocket foreshortened and dwindled into the sky. Less than a minute later, only the twisting vapor-trail was left.

"In 1942," continued the narrator, "the first of the great modern rockets was launched in secret from the Baltic shore. This was V.2, intended for the destruction of London. Since it was the prototype of all later machines, and of the spaceship itself, let us examine it in detail."

There followed a series of sectional drawings of V.2, showing all the essential components—the fuel tanks, the pumping system and the motor itself. By means of animated cartoons, the operation of the whole machine was demonstrated so clearly that no one could fail to understand it.

"V.2," continued the voice, "could reach altitudes of over one hundred miles, and after the War was used extensively for research into the ionosphere."

There were some spectacular shots of New Mexico firings in the late 1940's, and some even more spectacular ones of faulty take-offs and other forms of misbehavior.

"As you see, it was not always reliable and it was soon superseded by more powerful and readily controlled machines—such as these——"

The smooth torpedo-shape was being replaced by long, thin needles that went whistling up into the sky and came floating back beneath billowing parachutes. One after another speed and altitude records were being smashed. And in 1959 . . .

"This is the 'Orphan Annie' being assembled. She consisted of four separate stages, or 'steps,' each dropping off when its fuel supply was exhausted. Her initial weight was a hundred tons—her payload only twenty-five pounds. But that payload of magnesium powder was the first object from Earth to reach another world."

The Moon filled the screen, her craters glistening whitely and her long shadows lying, sharp and black, across the desolate plains. She was rather less than half full, and the ragged line of the terminator enclosed a great oval of darkness. Suddenly, in the heart of that hidden land, a tiny but brilliant spark of light flared for a moment and was gone. "Orphan Annie" had achieved her destiny.

"But all these rockets were pure projectiles: no human being had yet risen above the atmosphere and returned safely to Earth. The first manned machine, carrying a single pilot to an altitude of two hundred miles, was the 'Aurora Australis,' which was launched in 1962. By this time all long-range rocket research was based upon the great proving-grounds built in the Australian desert.

"After the 'Aurora' came other and more powerful ships, and in 1970, Lonsdale and McKinley, in an American machine, made the first orbital flights around the world, circling it three times before landing."

There was a breathtaking sequence, obviously speeded up many times, showing almost the whole Earth spinning below at an enormous rate. It made Dirk quite dizzy for a moment, and when he had recovered the narrator was talking about the force of gravity. He explained how it held everything to the Earth, and how it weakened with distance but never vanished completely. More animated diagrams showed how a body could be given such a speed that it would circle the world forever, balancing gravity against centrifugal force just as the Moon does in its own orbit. This was illustrated by a man whirling a stone around his head at the end of a piece of string. Slowly he lengthened the string, but still kept the stone circling, more and more slowly.

"Near the Earth," explained the voice, "bodies have

to travel at five miles a second to remain in stable or-bits—but the Moon, a quarter of a million miles away in a much weaker gravitational field, need move at only a tenth of this speed.

"But what happens if a body, such as a rocket, leaves the Earth at *more* than five miles a second? Watch . . ."

A model of the Earth appeared, floating in space. Above the equator a tiny point was moving, tracing out a circular path.

"Here is a rocket, traveling at five miles a second just outside the atmosphere. You will see that its path is a perfect circle. Now, if we increase its speed to *six* miles a second the rocket still travels round the Earth in a closed orbit, but its path has become an ellipse. As the speed increases still further, the ellipse becomes longer and longer and the rocket goes far out into space. But it aways returns.

"However, if we increase the rocket's initial speed to seven miles a second the ellipse becomes a parabola —so—and the rocket has escaped for ever. Earth's gravity can never recapture it: it is now traveling through space like a tiny, man-made comet. If the Moon were in the right position, our rocket would crash into it like the 'Orphan Annie.' "

That, of course, was the last thing one wanted a spaceship to do. There was a long explanation then, showing all the stages of a hypothetical lunar voyage. The commentator showed how much fuel must be car-ried for a safe landing, and how much more was needed for a safe return. He touched lightly on the problems of navigation in space, and explained how provision could be made for the safety of the crew. Finally he ended:

"With chemically propelled rockets we have achieved much, but to conquer space, and not merely to make short-lived raids into it, we must harness the limitless forces of atomic energy. At present, atomi-cally driven rockets are still in their infancy: they are dangerous and uncertain. But within a few years we shall have perfected them, and mankind will have taken its first great stride along the Road to Space."

The voice had grown louder; there was a throbbing background of music. Then Dirk seemed to be suspended motionless in space, a few hundred feet from the ground. There was just time for him to pick out a few scattered buildings and to realize that he was in a rocket that had just been launched. Then the sense of time returned: the desert began to drop away, with accelerating speed. A range of low hills came into view and was instantly foreshortened into flatness. The picture was slowly rotating, and abruptly a coastline cut across his field of vision. The scale contracted remorselessly, and with a sudden shock he realized that he was now seeing the whole coast of Southern Austrailia.

The rocket was no longer accelerating, but was sweeping away from Earth at a speed not far short of escape velocity. The twin islands of New Zealand swam into view—and then, at the edge of the picture, appeared a line of whiteness which for a moment he thought was a cloud.

Something seemed to catch at Dirk's throat when he realized that he was looking down upon the eternal icewalls of the Antarctic. He remembered the *Discovery,* moored not half a mile away. His eye could encompass in a moment the whole of the land over which Scott and his companions, less than a lifetime ago, had struggled and died.

And then the edge of the world reared up before him. The wonderfully efficient gyro-stabilization was beginning to fail and the camera wandered away into space. For a long time, it seemed, there was blackness and night; then, without warning, the camera came full upon the sun and the screen was blasted with light.

When the Earth returned, he could see the entire hemisphere spread beneath him. The picture froze once more and the music stilled, so that he had time to pick out the continents and oceans on that remote and unfamiliar world below.

For long minutes that distant globe hung there before his eyes; then, slowly, it dissolved. The lesson was over, but he would not soon forget it.

7

On the whole, Dirk's relations with the two young draftsmen who shared the office were cordial. They were not quite sure of his official position (that, he sometimes thought, made three of them) and so treated him with an odd mixture of deference and familiarity. There was one respect, however, in which they annoyed him intensely.

It seemed to Dirk that there were only two attitudes to adopt towards interplanetary flight. Either one was for it, or one was against it. What he could not understand was a position of complete indifference. These youngsters (he himself, of course, was a good five years older) earning their living in the very heart of Interplanetary itself, did not seem to have the slightest interest in the project. They drew their plans and made their calculations just as enthusiastically as if they were preparing drawings for washing machines instead of spaceships. They were, however, prepared to show traces of vivacity when defending their attitudes.

"The trouble with you, Doc," said the elder, Sam, one afternoon, "is that you take life too seriously. It doesn't pay. Bad for the arteries and that sort of thing."

"Unless some people did a bit of worrying," retorted Dirk, "there'd be no jobs for lazy so-and-sos like you and Bert."

"What's wrong with that?" said Bert. "They ought to be grateful. If it wasn't for chaps like Sam and me, they'd have nothing to worry about and would die of frustration. Most of 'em do, anyway."

Sam shifted his cigarette. (Did he use glue to keep it dangling from his lower lip at that improbable angle?)

"You're always agitating about the past, which is dead and done with, or the future, which we won't be around to see. Why not relax and enjoy yourself for a change?"

"I *am* enjoying myself," said Dirk. "I don't suppose you realize that there are people who happen to like work."

"They kid themselves into thinking they do," explained Bert. "It's all a matter of conditioning. We were smart enough to dodge it."

"I think," said Dirk admiringly, "that if you keep on devoting so much energy to concocting excuses to avoid work, you'll evolve a new philosophy. The philosophy of Futilitarianism."

"Did you make that up on the spur of the moment?"

"No," confessed Dirk.

"I thought not. Sounded as if you'd been saving it up."

"Tell me," Dirk asked, "don't you feel any intellectual curiosity about anything?"

"Not particularly, as long as I know where my next pay check's coming from."

They were pulling his leg, of course, and they knew he knew it. Dirk laughed and went on:

"It seems to me that Public Relations has overlooked a nice little oasis of inertia right on its own doorstep. Why, I don't believe you care a hoot whether the 'Prometheus' reaches the Moon or not!"

"I wouldn't say that," protested Sam. "I've got a fiver on her."

Before Dirk could think of a suitably blistering reply, the door was thrown open and Matthews appeared. Sam and Bert, with smoothly co-ordinated motions that eluded the eye, were instantly hard at work among their drawings.

Matthews was obviously in a hurry.

"Want a free tea?" he said.

"It depends. Where?"

"House of Commons. You were saying the other day that you'd never been there."

"This sounds interesting. What's it all about?"

"Grab your things and I'll tell you on the way."

In the taxi, Matthews relaxed and explained.

"We often get jobs like this," he said. "Mac was supposed to be coming, but he's had to go to New York and won't be back for a couple of days. So I thought you might like to come along. For the record, you can be one of our legal advisers."

"This is very thoughtful of you," said Dirk gratefully. "Who are we going to see?"

"A dear old chap named Sir Michael Flannigan. He's an Irish Tory—very much so. Some of his constituents don't hold with these new-fangled spaceships —they've probably never really got used to the Wright Brothers. So we have to go along and explain what it's all about."

"No doubt you'll succeed in allaying his doubts," said Dirk as they drove past County Hall and turned on to Westminster Bridge.

"I hope so; I've got a line which I think should fix things very nicely."

They passed under the shadow of Big Ben and drove for a hundred yards along the side of the great Gothic building. The entrance at which they stopped was an inconspicuous archway leading into a long hall which seemed very remote from the bustle of traffic in the square outside. It was cool and quiet, and to Dirk the feeling of age and centuries-old traditions was overwhelming.

Climbing a short flight of steps, they found themselves in a large chamber from which corridors radiated in several directions. A small crowd was milling around, and people sat in expectant attitudes along wooden benches. On the right a reception desk was flanked by a stout policeman in full regalia, helmet and all.

Matthews walked up to the desk, and collected a form which he filled in and handed to the policeman. Nothing happened for some time. Then a uniformed official appeared, shouted a string of quite incomprehensible words, and gathered the forms from the policeman. He then vanished down one of the corridors.

"What on earth did he say?" hissed Dirk in the silence that had suddenly descended.

"He said that Mr. Jones, Lady Carruthers, and someone else whose name I couldn't catch, aren't in the House at the moment."

The message must have been generally understood, for groups of disgruntled constituents began to drift out of the chamber, foiled of their prey.

"Now we've got to wait," said Matthews, "but it shouldn't be long, as we're expected."

From time to time in the next ten minutes other names were called, and occasionally members arrived to collect their guests. Sometimes Matthews pointed out a notable of whom Dirk had never heard, though he did his best to disguise the fact.

Presently he noticed that the policeman was pointing them out to a tall young man who was very far from his conceptions of an elderly Irish baronet.

The young man came over to them.

"How do you do?" he said. "My name is Fox. Sir Michael is engaged for a few moments, so he asked me to look after you. Perhaps you'd care to listen to the debate until Sir Michael's free?"

"I'm sure we would," Matthews replied, a little too heartily. Dirk guessed that the experience was not particularly novel to him, but he was delighted at the chance of witnessing Parliament in action.

They followed their guide through interminable corridors and beneath numberless archways. Finally he handed them over to an ancient attendant who might very well have witnessed the signing of Magna Carta.

"He'll find you a good seat," promised Mr. Fox. "Sir Michael will be along for you in a few minutes."

They thanked him and followed the attendant up a winding stairway.

"Who was that?" asked Dirk.

"Robert Fox—Labour M.P. for Taunton," explained Matthews. "That's one thing about the House —everyone always helps everybody else. Parties don't matter as much as outsiders might think." He turned to the attendant.

"What's being debated now?"

"The Second Reading of the Soft Drinks (Control) Bill," said the ancient in a funereal voice.

"Oh, dear!" said Matthews. "Let's hope it *is* only for a few minutes!"

The benches high in the gallery gave them a good view of the debating chamber. Photographs had made his surroundings quite familiar to Dirk, but he had always pictured a scene of animation with members rising to cry "On a point of order!" or, better still, "Shame!" "Withdraw!" and other Parliamentary noises. Instead, he saw about thirty languid gentlemen draped along the benches while a junior minister read a not-very-enthralling schedule of prices and profits. While he watched, two members simultaneously decided that they had had enough and, with little curtseys to the Speaker, hastily withdrew—no doubt, thought Dirk, in search of drinks that were not particularly soft.

His attention wandered from the scene below and he examined the great chamber around him. It seemed very well preserved for its age, and it was wonderful to think of the historic scenes it had witnessed down the centuries, right back to——

"Looks pretty good, doesn't it?" whispered Matthews. "It was only finished in 1950, you know."

Dirk came back to earth with a bump.

"Good heavens! I thought it was centuries old!"

"Oh, no: Hitler wrote off the earlier chamber in the Blitz."

Dirk felt rather annoyed with himself for not remembering this, and turned his attention once more to the debate. There were now fifteen members present on the Government side, while the Conservative and Labour parties on the Opposition benches could only muster a baker's dozen between them.

The paneled door against which they were sitting opened abruptly, and a smiling round face beamed at them. Matthews shot to his feet as their host greeted them with many apologies. Out in the corridor, where voices could be raised again, introductions were effected and they followed Sir Michael through yet more passages to the restaurant. Dirk decided that he had never seen so many acres of wooden paneling in his life.

The old baronet must have been well over seventy, but he walked with a springy step and his complexion was almost cherubic. His tonsured pate made the resemblance to some medieval abbot so striking that Dirk felt he had just stepped into Glastonbury or Wells before the dissolution of the monasteries. Yet if he closed his eyes, Sir Michael's accent transported him instantly to metropolitan New York. The last time he had encountered a brogue like that, its owner had been handing him a ticket for passing a "Stop" sign.

They sat down to tea and Dirk carefully declined the offer of coffee. During the meal they discussed trivialities and avoided the object of the meeting. It was only broached when they had moved out on to the long terrace flanking the Thames which, Dirk could not help thinking, was a scene of much greater activity than the debating chamber itself. Little groups of people stood or sat around, talking briskly, and there was much coming and going of messengers. Sometimes the members would, *en masse,* disengage themselves apologetically from their guests and dash off to register their votes. During one of these lacunae, Matthews did his best to make Parliamentary procedure clear to Dirk.

"You'll realize," he said, "that most of the work is done in the committee rooms. Except during important debates, only the specialists or the members who are particularly interested are actually in the Chamber. The others are working on reports or seeing constituents in their little cubbyholes all over the building."

"Now, boys," boomed Sir Michael as he returned, having collected a tray of drinks on the way, "tell me about this scheme of yours for going to the Moon."

Matthews cleared his throat, and Dirk pictured his mind running rapidly through all the possible opening gambits.

"Well, Sir Michael," he began, "it's only a logical extension of what mankind's been doing since history began. For thousands of years the human race has been spreading over the world until the whole globe has been explored and colonized. The time's now come to make the next step and to cross space to the other planets. Humanity must always have new frontiers, new horizons. Otherwise it will sooner or later sink back into decadence. Interplanetary travel's the next stage in our development, and it will be wise to take it before it's forced upon us by shortage of raw materials or space. And there are also psychological reasons for space flight. Many years ago someone likened our little Earth to a goldfish bowl inside which the human mind couldn't keep circling forever with stagnation. The world was big enough for mankind in the days of the stagecoach and the sailing ship, but it's far too small now that we can round it in a couple of hours."

Matthews leaned back to watch the effect of his shock tactics. For a moment Sir Michael looked a little dazed: then he made a quick recovery and downed the remainder of his drink.

"It's all a little overwhelming," he said ruefully.

"But what will you do when you get to the Moon, anyway?"

"You must realize," said Matthews, pressing on remorselessly, "that the Moon's only the beginning. Fifteen million square miles is quite a good beginning, to be sure, but we only look upon it as a stepping-stone to the planets. As you know, there's no free air or water there, so the first colonies will have to be totally enclosed. But the low gravity will make it easy to build very large structures and plans have been drawn up for whole cities under great transparent domes."

"Seems to me," said Sir Michael shrewdly, "that you're going to take your 'goldfish bowls' with you!"

Matthews nearly smiled.

"A good point," he conceded, "but probably the Moon will be mainly used by the astronomers and physicists for scientific research. It's enormously important to them, and whole new areas of knowledge will be opened up when they can build labs and observatories up there."

"And will that make the world a better or a happier place?"

"That, as always, depends on humanity. Knowledge is neutral, but one *must* possess it to do either good or ill."

Matthews waved his arm along the great river moving sluggishly past them between its crowded banks.

"Everything you can see, everything in our modern world, is possible because of the knowledge which men won in ancient times. And civilization isn't static: if it stands still, it will die."

There was silence for a while. Almost in spite of himself, Dirk felt deeply impressed. He wondered if he had been wrong in thinking that Matthews was merely an efficient salesman, propagating the ideals of others. Was he no more than a talented instrumentalist, performing a piece of music with complete technical skill but without any real feeling? He could not be sure. Matthews, extrovert though he was, concealed depths of reserve which Dirk could never plumb. In this, though in no other respect, he filled the specifications of that fabulous creature, the typical Englishman.

"I've had a good many letters," said Sir Michael presently, "from friends of mine in Ireland who don't like the idea at all and think we were never intended to leave the Earth. What am I to say to them?"

"Remind them of history," replied Matthews. "Tell them that we're explorers, and ask them not to forget that once upon a time *someone* had to discover Ireland!" He gave Dirk a glance as if to say: "Here it comes."

"Imagine that it's five centuries ago, Sir Michael, and that my name's Christopher Columbus. You want to know why I'm anxious to sail westward across the Atlantic, and I've tried to give you my reasons. I don't know whether they've convinced you: you may not be particularly interested in opening up a new route to the Indies. But this is the important point—neither of us can imagine just how much this voyage is going to mean to the world. *Tell your friends, Sir Michael, to think what a difference it would have made to Ireland if America had never been discovered.* The Moon's a bigger place than North and South America combined—and it's only the first and smallest of the worlds we're going to reach."

The great reception hall was almost deserted when they said good-bye to Sir Michael. He still seemed a trifle dazed when they shook hands and parted.

"I hope that settles the Irish question for a while," said Matthews as they walked out of the building into the shadow of the Victoria Tower. "What did you think of the old boy?"

"He seemed a grand character. I'd give a lot to

hear him explaining your ideas to his constituents."

"Yes," Matthews replied, "that should be rather entertaining."

They walked on for a couple of yards, past the main entrance and toward the bridge. Then Matthews said abruptly:

"What do *you* think of it all, anyway?"

Dirk hedged.

"I think I agree with you—logically," he said. "But somehow I can't feel about it the way you seem to do. Later, perhaps, I may—I just can't tell."

He looked at the great city around him, throbbing with life and commerce. It seemed as ageless and eternal as the hills: whatever the future brought, surely this could never pass away! Yet Matthews had been right, and he of all people should recognize it. Civilization could never stand still. Over the very ground on which he was walking, the mammoths had once come trampling through the rushes at the river's edge. They, and not the ape-men watching from their caves, had been the masters of this land. But the day of the ape had dawned at last: the forests and swamps had given way before the might of his machines. Dirk knew now that the story was merely beginning. Even at this moment, on far worlds beneath strange suns, Time and the Gods were preparing for Man the sites of cities yet to be.

8

Sir Robert Derwent, M.A., F.R.S., Director-General of Interplanetary, was a rather tough-looking character who invariably reminded people of the late Winston Churchill. The resemblance was somewhat spoiled by his addiction to pipes, of which, according to rumor, he possessed two varieties—"Normal" and "Emergency." The "Emergency" model was always kept fully fuelled so that it could be brought into action at once when unwelcome visitors arrived. The secret mixture used for this purpose was believed to consist largely of sulphureted tea leaves.

Sir Robert was such a striking personality that a host of legends had grown up around him. Many of these had been concocted by his assistants, who would have gone through Hell for their chief—and frequently did, since his command of language was not that normally expected of an ex-Astronomer Royal. He was no respecter of persons or proprieties, and some of his retorts to famous but not excessively intelligent questioners had become historic. Even Royalty had been glad to disengage itself from his fire on one celebrated occasion. Yet despite all this façade, he was at heart a kindly and sensitive person. A good many people suspected this, but very few had ever been able to prove it to their satisfaction.

At the age of sixty, and three times a grandfather, Sir Robert appeared to be a rather well-preserved forty-five. Like his historic double, he attributed this to a careful neglect of all the elementary rules of health and a steady intake of nicotine. A brilliant reporter had once aptly called him "A scientific Francis Drake—one of the astronomical explorers of the Second Elizabethan Age."

There was nothing very Elizabethan about the Director-General as he sat reading the day's mail beneath a faint nimbus of tobacco smoke. He dealt with his correspondence at an astonishing rate, stacking the letters in small piles as he finished them. From time to time he filed a communication directly into the wastepaper basket, from which his staff would carefully retrieve it for inclusion in a voluminous folder with the elegant title "NUTS." About one per cent of Interplanetary's incoming mail came under this category.

He had just finished when the office door opened and Dr. Groves, Interplanetary's psychological adviser, came in with a file of reports. Sir Robert looked at him morosely.

"Well, you bird of ill-omen—what's all this fuss about young Hassell? I thought that everything was under control."

Groves looked worried as he laid down the folder.

"So did I, until a few weeks ago. Until then all five of the boys were shaping well and showing no signs of strain. Then we noticed that Vic was being worried by something, and I finally had it out with him yesterday."

"It's his wife, I suppose?"

"Yes. The whole thing's very unfortunate. Vic's just the sort of father who gives trouble at the best of times, and Maude Hassell doesn't know that he'll probably be on his way to the Moon when the boy arrives."

The D.-G. raised his eyebrows.

"You know it's a boy?"

"The Weismann-Mathers treatment is ninety-five per cent certain. Vic wanted a son—just in case he didn't get back."

"I see. How do you think Mrs. Hassell will react when she knows? Of course, it still isn't certain that Vic *is* going to be in the crew."

"I think she'll be all right. But Vic's the one who's worrying. How did you feel when *your* first kid arrived?"

Sir Robert grinned.

"That's digging into the past. As it happens, I was away myself—on an eclipse expedition. I very nearly smashed a coronograph, so I understand Vic's point of view. But it's a damned nuisance; you'll just have to reason with him. Tell him to have it out with his wife, but ask her not to say anything. Are there any other complications likely to arise?"

"Not that I can foresee. But you never can tell."

"No, you can't, can you?"

The Director-General's eyes strayed to the little

motto in its frame at the back of his desk. Dr. Groves could not see them from where he sat, but he knew the lines by heart and they had often intrigued him:

> *"There is always a thing forgotten*
> *Whenever the world goes well."*

One day, he'd have to ask where that came from.

Part Two

Two hundred and seventy miles above the Earth, "Beta" was making her third circuit of the globe. Skirting the atmosphere like a tiny satellite, she was completing one revolution every ninety minutes. Unless the pilot turned on her motors again, she would remain here forever, on the frontiers of space.

Yet, "Beta" was a creature of the upper atmosphere rather than the deeps of space. Like those fish which sometimes clamber on to the land, she was venturing outside her true element, and her great wings were now useless sheets of metal burning beneath the savage sun. Not until she returned to the air far beneath would they be of any service again

Fixed upon "Beta's" back was a streamlined torpedo that might, at first glance, have been taken for another rocket. But there were no observation ports, no motor nozzles, no signs of landing gear. The sleek metal shape was almost featureless, like a giant bomb awaiting the moment of release. It was the first of the fuel containers for "Alpha," holding tons of liquid methane which would be pumped into the spaceship's tanks when it was ready to make its voyage.

"Beta" seemed to be hanging motionless against the ebon sky, while the Earth itself turned beneath her. The technicians aboard the ship, checking their in-

51

struments and relaying their findings to the control stations on the planet below, were in no particular hurry. It made little difference to them whether they circled the Earth once or a dozen times. They would stay in their orbit until they were satisfied with their tests—unless, as the chief engineer had remarked, they were forced down earlier by a shortage of cigarettes.

Presently, minute puffs of gas spurted along the line of contact between "Beta" and the fuel tank upon her back. The explosive bolts connecting them had been sheared: very slowly, at the rate of a few feet a minute, the great tank began to drift away from the ship.

In the hull of "Beta" an airlock door opened and two men floated out in their unwieldy spacesuits. With short bursts of gas from tiny cylinders, they directed themselves toward the drifting fuel tank and began to inspect it carefully. One of them opened a little hatch and started to take instrument readings, while the other began a survey of the hull with a portable leak detector.

Nothing else happened for nearly an hour, apart from occasional spurts of vapor from "Beta's" auxiliary steering jets. The pilot was turning her so that she pointed against her orbital motion, and was obviously taking his time over the maneuver. A distance of nearly a hundred feet now lay between "Beta" and the fuel tank she had carried up from Earth. It was hard to realize that during their slow separation the two bodies had almost circled the Earth.

The space-suited engineers had finished their task. Slowly they jetted back to the waiting ship and the airlock door closed again behind them. There was another long pause as the pilot waited for the exact moment to begin braking.

Quite suddenly, a stream of unbearable incandescence jetted from "Beta's" stern. The white-hot gases seemed to form a solid bar of light. To the men in the ship, normal weight would have returned again as the motors started to thrust. Every five seconds, "Beta" was losing a hundred miles an hour of her speed. She *was breaking her orbit, and would soon be falling back to Earth.*

The intolerable flame of the atomic rocket flickered and died. Once more the little controlling jets spurted vapor: the pilot was in a hurry now as he swung the ship round on her axis again. Out in space, one orientation was as good as another—but in a few minutes the ship would be entering atmosphere and must be pointing in the direction of her motion.

It would always be a tense moment, waiting for that first contact. To the men in the ship, it came in the form of a gentle but irresistible tugging of their seat-straps. Slowly it increased, minute by minute, until presently there came the faintest whisper of sound through the insulation of the walls. They were trading altitude for speed—speed which they could only lose against air-resistance. If the rate of exchange was too great, the stubby wings would snap, the hull would turn to molten metal, and the ship would crash in meteoric ruin down through a hundred miles of sky.

The wings were biting again into the thin air streaming past them at eighteen thousand miles an hour. Although the control surfaces were still useless, the ship would soon be responding sluggishly to their commands. Even without the use of his engines, the pilot could choose a landing spot almost anywhere on Earth. He was flying a hypersonic glider whose speed had given it world-wide range.

Very slowly, the ship was settling down through the stratosphere, losing speed minute by minute. At little more than a thousand miles an hour, the air-scoops of the ramjets were opened and the atomic furnaces began to glow with deadly life. Streams of burning air were being blasted from the nozzles and in its wake the ship was leaving the familiar reddish-brown tinge of nitric oxides. It was riding the atmosphere again, safely under power, and could turn once more for home.

The final test was over. Almost three hundred miles above, exchanging night and day every forty minutes, the first fuel tank was spinning in its eternal orbit. In a few days its companions would be launched in the same path, by the same means. They would be lashed together, awaiting the moment when they would pour their contents into the empty tanks of "Alpha" and speed the spaceship on the journey to the Moon. . . .

1

As Matthews put it, the "Department of Negative Publicity" had gone into forward gear at last—and once started, it changed rapidly into top. The successful launching of the first fuel container, and the safe return of "Beta" showed that everything that could be checked was functioning perfectly. The now fully trained crew would be leaving for Australia in a few days, and the need for secrecy was past.

A hilarious morning was spent at Southbank as the press reports of the first visit to the "Nursery" came in. The science editors of the great dailies had, as usual, produced reasonably accurate accounts: but some of the smaller papers, who had sent along sports reporters, dramatic critics, or anyone else who happened to be handy, had printed some truly marvelous stories. Matthews spent most of the day in a state of mingled mirth and mortification, launching a telephonic barrage in the general direction of Fleet Street. Dirk warned him that it would be wise to save most of his indignation for the arrival of the transatlantic press reports.

Hassell, Leduc, Clinton, Richards and Taine promptly became the targets of almost unparalleled curiosity. Their life-stories (thoughtfully mimeographed well in advance by Public Relations) were promptly serialized in newspapers all over the word. Offers of matrimony poured in by every post, descending impartially upon the married and the unmarried men alike. Begging letters also arrived in hordes: as

Richards remarked wryly: "Everyone except life-insurance agents wants to sell us *something.*"

The affairs of Interplanetary were now moving toward their climax with the smoothness of a military operation. In a week, the crew and all the higher staff would be leaving for Australia. With them would go everyone else who could possibly think of a suitable excuse. During the next few days many preoccupied expressions were to be seen around the building. Junior clerks had a habit of suddenly discovering sick aunts in Sydney or impecunious cousins in Canberra who required their presence immediately.

The idea of the farewell party had, it seemed, originated in the Director-General's mind and had been enthusiastically taken up by McAndrews, who was annoyed at not having thought of it himself. All the headquarters staff was to be invited, as well as large numbers of people from industry, the press, the universities, and the innumerable organizations with which Interplanetary had dealings. After much whittling of lists and a good deal of heartburning, just over seven hundred invitations had been sent out. Even the Chief Accountant, still boggling at the thought of a two-thousand-pound "hospitality" item, had been brought to heel by threats of exclusion.

There were a few who thought that these celebrations were premature and it would be better to wait until the "Prometheus" returned. To these critics it was pointed out that many of the workers on the project would not be returning to London after the launch, but would be going back to their own countries. This was the last opportunity of getting them all together. Pierre Leduc summed up the crew's attitude when he said: "If we come back, we'll have enough parties then to last us the rest of our lives. If we *don't,* then you ought to give us a good send-off."

The hotel selected for the bacchanalia was one of the best in London, but not one so good that only a few of the executives and practically none of the scientists would feel at ease. Speeches, it had been solemnly promised, would be kept to a minimum to leave as much time as possible for the proper business. This suited Dirk, who had a hatred for orations but a considerable fondness for banquets and buffets.

He arrived ten minutes before the official time, and found Matthews pacing up and down the foyer, flanked by a couple of muscular waiters. He indicated them without a smile.

"My strong-arm men," he said. "Look carefully, and you can see the bulges in their hip-pockets. We expect lots of gate-crashers, particularly from the section of Fleet Street we haven't invited. I'm afraid you'll have to look after yourself tonight, but the chaps with 'Steward' on their lapels will tell you who's who if there's anyone you want to meet."

"That's all right," said Dirk, checking his hat and coat. "I hope you get time to have a snack now and then while you're holding the fort."

"My emergency reserves are well organized. You'll get your drinks, by the way, from the chaps labeled 'Fuel Technician.' We've called all the drinks after some rocket fuel or other, so no one will know what they've got until they drink it—if then. But I'll give you a tip."

"What's that?"

"Lay off the hydrazine hydrate!"

"Thanks for the warning," laughed Dirk. He was somewhat relieved to find, a few minutes later, that Matthews had been pulling his leg and that no such disguises had been employed.

The place filled rapidly in the next half-hour. Dirk did not know more than one person in twenty, and felt a little out in the cold. Consequently he kept somewhat nearer the bar than was altogether good for him. From time to time he nodded to acquaintances, but most of them were too fully engaged elsewhere to join him. He was rather glad when another equally unattached guest settled down beside him in search of company.

They got into conversation in a somewhat desultory

manner, and after a while the talk came around, inevitably, to the approaching adventure.

"By the way," said the stranger, "I've not seen you around Interplanetary before. Have you been here long?"

"Only three weeks or so," said Dirk. "I'm on a special job for the University of Chicago."

"Indeed?"

Dirk felt talkative, and the other seemed to show a flattering interest in his affairs.

"I've got to write the official history of the first voyage and the events leading up to it. This trip is going to be one of the most important things that's ever happened, and it's necessary to have a complete record for the future."

"But surely there'll be thousands of technical reports and newspaper accounts?"

"Quite true: but you forget that they'll be written for contemporaries and will assume a background which may only be familiar to present-day readers. I have to try and stand outside of Time, as it were, and produce a record which can be read with full understanding ten thousand years from today."

"Phew! Some job!"

"Yes: it's only become possible recently through the new developments in the study of language and meaning, and the perfection of symbolic vocabularies. But I'm afraid I'm boring you."

To his annoyance, the other didn't contradict him.

"I suppose," said the stranger casually, "you've got to know the people round here pretty well. I mean, you're in rather a privileged position."

"That's true: they've looked after me excellently and helped me all they could."

"There goes young Hassell," said his companion. "He looks a bit worried, but so would I in his shoes. Have you got to know the crew at all well?"

"Not yet, though I hope to do so. I've spoken to Hassell and Leduc a couple of times, but that's all."

"Who do you think's going to be chosen for the trip?"

Dirk was about to give his not-very-well-informed views on this subject when he saw Matthews frantically signaling to him from the other side of the room. For a moment alarming possibilities of sartorial disaster raced through his mind. Then a slow suspicion dawned, and with a mumbled excuse he disengaged himself from his companion.

A few moments later, Matthews confirmed his fears.

"Mike Wilkins is one of the best—we used to work together on the *News*. But for goodness' sake be careful what you say to him. If you'd murdered your wife he'd get it out of you by asking leading questions about the weather."

"Still, I don't think there's much I could tell him that he doesn't know already."

"Don't you believe it. Before you know where you are, you'll be featured in the paper as 'an important official of Interplanetary' and I'll be sending out the usual ineffective disclaimers."

"I see. How many other reporters have we got among our guests?"

"About twelve were *invited*," said Matthews darkly. "I should just avoid all heart-to-heart talks with people you don't know. Excuse me now—I must go back on guard duty."

As far as he was concerned, thought Dirk, the party was hardly going with a swing. The Public Relations Department seemed to have an obsession about security, which Dirk considered they had pushed to extremes. However, he could understand Matthews' horror of unofficial interviews—he had seen some of their gruesome results.

For quite a time after this Dirk's attention was fully occupied by an astonishingly pretty girl who appeared to have arrived without an escort—a fact somewhat surprising in itself. He had just, after much vacillation, decided to step into the breach when it became all too obvious that the escort had merely been engaged on convoy duties elsewhere. Dirk hadn't missed his opportunity: he had never had one. He turned once more to philosophical musings.

His spirits, however, revived considerably during dinner. The meal itself was excellent and even the Director-General's speech (which set a limit for all the others) only lasted ten minutes. It was, as far as Dirk could remember, an extremely witty address full of private jokes which produced roars of laughter in some quarters and sickly smiles in others. Interplanetary had always been fond of laughing at itself in private, but only recently could it afford the luxury of doing so in public.

The remaining few orations were even shorter: several speakers would clearly have liked more time, but dared not take it. Finally McAndrews, who had acted throughout as a very efficient Master of Ceremonies, called a toast for the success of the "Prometheus" and her crew.

Afterwards there was much dancing to the gentle, nostalgic rhythms so popular in the late '70s. Dirk, who was a very bad dancer at the best of times, made several erratic circuits with Mrs. Matthews and the wives of other officials before an increasing lack of muscular co-ordination warned him off the field. He then sat watching the proceedings through a benevolent glow, thinking what nice people all his friends were and tut-tutting slightly when he noticed dancers who had obviously taken aboard just a little too much "fuel."

It must have been around midnight when he suddenly became aware that someone was speaking to him. (He hadn't been asleep, of course, but it was refreshing to close one's eyes now and then.) He turned sluggishly and found a tall, middle-aged man watching him with some amusement from the next chair. To Dirk's surprise, he was not in evening dress and did not seem to be worried by the fact.

"I saw your fraternity badge," said the other by way of introduction. "I'm Sigma Xi myself. Only got back from California this evening—too late for the dinner."

So that explained the dress, thought Dirk, feeling rather pleased with himself at so brilliant a piece of deduction. He shook hands, glad to meet a fellow Californian—though he couldn't catch the name. It seemed to be something like Mason, but it didn't really matter.

For some time they discussed American affairs and speculated on the Democrats' chances of returning to power. Dirk contended that the Liberals would once again hold the balance, and made some brilliant comments on the advantages and disadvantages of the three-party system. Strangely enough, his companion seemed unimpressed by his wit, and brought the conversation back to Interplanetary.

"You haven't been here very long, have you?" he queried. "How are you getting on?"

Dirk told him, at length. He explained his job, and enlarged lavishly upon its scope and importance. When he had finished his work, all subsequent eras and all possible planets would realize exactly what the conquest of space had meant to the age which had achieved it.

His friend seemed very interested, though there was a trace of amusement in his voice about which Dirk might have to reprimand him, gently but firmly.

"How have you got on in your contacts with the technical side?" he asked.

"To tell the truth," said Dirk sadly, "I've been intending to do something about this for the last week. But I'm rather scared of scientists, you know. Besides, there's Matthews. He's been very helpful, but he has his own ideas of what I should do and I'm anxious not to hurt his feelings."

That was a deplorably weak sort of statement, but there was a lot of truth in it. Matthews had organized everything a little too completely.

Thinking of Alfred brought back memories, and Dirk was filled with a sudden grave suspicion. He looked carefully at his companion, determined not to be caught again.

The fine profile and the wide, intelligent brow were reassuring, but Dirk was now too old a hand at the game to be deceived. Alfred, he thought, would be proud of the way he was evading definite answers to his companion's queries. It was rather a pity, of course, since the other was a fellow American and had come a long way in search of a "scoop"; still, his first loyalty now was with his hosts.

The other must have realized that he was getting nowhere, for presently he rose to his feet and gave Dirk a quizzical smile.

"I think," he said, as he took his leave, "that I may be able to put you in touch with the right people on the technical side. Ring me tomorrow at Extension 3—don't forget—3."

Then he was gone, leaving Dirk in a highly confused state of mind. His fears, it seemed, had been groundless: the fellow belonged to Interplanetary after all. Oh well, it couldn't be helped.

His next clear recollection was saying good-night to Matthews in the foyer. Alfred still seemed annoyingly bright and energetic, and very pleased with the success of the party—though it seemed that he had suffered from qualms from time to time.

"During that horn-pipe," he said, "I was quite certain that the floor was going to give way. Do you realize that would have delayed the conquest of space by at least half a century?"

Dirk did not feel particularly interested in such metaphysical speculations, but as he bade a sleepy good-night he suddenly remembered his unknown Californian.

"By the way," he said, "I got talking with another American—thought he was a journalist at first. He'd just arrived in town—you must have seen him—he wasn't wearing evening dress. Told me to ring him tomorrow at extension something-or-other. Know who he was?"

Matthews's eyes twinkled.

"You thought he was another journalist, did you? I hope you remembered my warning."

"Yes," said Dirk proudly. "I never told him a thing. Though it wouldn't have mattered, would it?"

Matthews pushed him into the cab and slammed the door. He leaned through the window for his parting words.

"No, it certainly wouldn't," he said. "That was only Professor Maxton, the Deputy Director-General. Go home and sleep it off!"

2

Dirk managed to arrive at the office in time for lunch —a meal which, he noticed, did not seem very popular. He had never seen so few customers in the canteen before.

When he rang up Extension 3 and introduced himself sheepishly, Professor Maxton seemed glad to hear him and invited him round at once. He found the Deputy D.-G. in the next office to Sir Robert Derwent, almost surrounded with packing cases—holding, he explained, special test gear which was to be flown to Australia at once. Their conversation was frequently interrupted by the Professor's orders and counter-orders to his perspiring assistants as they checked through their equipment.

"I'm sorry if I seemed a bit offhand last night," said Dirk apologetically. "The fact is, I wasn't quite myself."

"I gathered that," said Maxton dryly. "After all, you had several hours' start on me! Hi, you dope, don't carry that recorder upside down! Sorry, Alexson, I didn't mean you."

He paused for breath.

"This is an infernal business—you never know what you'll want and you can be pretty sure that in the end the most important stuff will get left behind."

"What's it all for?" asked Dirk, quite overcome by the arrays of glittering equipment and the sight of more radio tubes than he had ever seen before at any one time in his life.

"Post-mortem gear," said Maxton succinctly. " 'Alpha's' main instrument readings are telemetered back to Earth. If anything goes wrong, at least we'll know what happened."

"This isn't very cheerful talk after last night's gaiety."

"No, but it's practical talk and may save millions of dollars, as well as a good many lives. I've heard all about your project in the States, and thought it was a very interesting idea. Who started it?"

"The Rockefeller Foundation—History and Records Division."

"I'm glad the historians have finally realized that science does play quite a part in shaping the world. When I was a kid their textbooks were nothing but military primers. Then the economic determinists held the field—until the neo-Freudians routed them with great slaughter. We've only just got that lot under control—so let's hope we're going to get a balanced view at last."

"That's exactly what I'm aiming at," said Dirk. "I realize that all sorts of motives must have inspired the man who founded Interplanetary. I want to unravel and analyze them as far as possible. On the factual side, I've been supplied with everything I want by Matthews."

"Matthews? Oh, the chap from Public Relations. They think they run the place—don't believe everything they tell you, especially about us."

Dirk laughed.

"I thought that Interplanetary was all one big, happy family!"

"On the whole we get along pretty well, especially at the top. At least, we present a united front to the outside world. As a class, I think scientists work together better than any other, especially when they have a common goal. But you always have clashing personalities, and there seems an inevitable rivalry between the technical and the non-technical grades. Sometimes it's just good-natured fun, but often there's a certain amount of bitterness behind it."

While Maxon was speaking, Dirk had been studying him carefully. His first impression had been confirmed. The D.D.-G. was not only a man of obvious brilliance, but one of wide culture and sympathies. Dirk wondered how he got on with his equally brilliant but ferociously forthright colleague, Sir Robert. Two such contrasting personalities would either work together very well—or not at all.

At the age of fifty, Professor Maxton was generally regarded as the world's leading atomic engineer. He had played a major part in the development of nuclear propulsion systems for aircraft, and the drive units of the "Prometheus" were based almost entirely on his designs. The fact that such a man, who could have demanded almost any price from industry, was willing to work here at a nominal salary, seemed to Dirk a very significant point.

Maxton called out to a fair-haired young man in the late twenties who was just passing.

"Come here a minute, Ray—I've got another job for you!"

The other approached with a rueful grin.

"I hope it's nothing tough. I've got a bit of a headache this morning."

The D.D.-G. grinned at Dirk but refrained, after an obvious struggle, from making any comment.

He introduced them briefly.

"Dr. Alexson—Ray Collins, my personal assistant. Ray's line is hyperdynamics—short, but only just, for hypersonic aerodynamics, in case you didn't know. Ray—Dr. Alexson's a history specialist, so I guess you wonder what he's doing here. He hopes to be the Gibbon of astronautics."

"Not the 'Decline and Fall of Interplanetary,' I hope! Pleased to meet you."

"I want you to help Dr. Alexson with any technical queries. I've only just rescued him from the clammy clutches of McAndrew's mob, so he'll probably have some pretty weird ideas about things."

He turned to survey the surrounding chaos, found that his assistants were undermining the precarious seat he had adopted, and shifted to another packing case.

"I'd better explain," he continued, "though you probably know it already, that our little technical empire has three main divisions. Ray here is one of the airborne experts; he's concerned with getting the ship safely through the atmosphere—in both directions—with the minimum of wear and tear. His section used to be looked down upon by the space-hounds, who regarded the atmosphere as just a nuisance. They've changed their tune now that we've shown them how to use the air as a free fuel supply—for the first part of the trip at least."

That was one of the hundred or so points that Dirk had never properly understood, and he made a mental note, putting it first on his list of questions.

"Then there are the astronomers and mathematicians, who form a tight little trade-union of their own —though they've suffered some pretty heavy infiltration from the electronics engineers with their calculating machines. They, of course, have to compute orbits and do our mathematical donkey-work, which is very extensive indeed. Sir Robert himself is in charge of their affairs.

"Finally there are the rocket engineers, bless 'em. You won't find many here, for they're nearly all in Australia.

"So that's the set-up, though I've neglected several groups like the communications and control people, and the medical experts. I'll turn you over to Ray now, and he'll look after you."

Dirk winced slightly at the phrase; he felt that rather

too many people had been "looking after him." Collins led him to a small office not far away where they sat down and exchanged cigarettes. After puffing thoughtfully for some time, the aerodynamicist jerked his thumb toward the door and remarked:

"What do you think of the Chief?"

"I'm a bit biased, you know; we're from the same State. He seems a most remarkable man—cultured as well as technically brilliant. It's not a usual combination. And he's been very helpful."

Collins began to wax enthusiastic.

"That's perfectly true. He's the best chap you could possibly work for, and I don't think he has a single enemy. That's quite a contrast to Sir Robert, who has dozens among people who know him only slightly."

"I've met the Director-General only once. I didn't know quite what to make of him."

Collins laughed.

"It takes a long time to get used to the D.-G.—he certainly hasn't Professor Maxton's easy charm. If you do a job badly, the D.-G. will burn your ears off while the Prof. will give you a hurt look that makes you feel like a professional baby-poisoner. Both techniques work perfectly, and everyone's very fond of Sir Robert when they get to know him."

Dirk examined the room with more than casual interest. It was a typical small drafting room with a modern internally illuminated tracing table occupying one corner. The walls were covered with elaborate and obscure graphs, interspersed with photographs of rockets removing themselves spectacularly to distant parts. A place of honor was given to a magnificent view of the Earth from a height of at least a thousand miles. Dirk guessed it was a still from the film that Matthews had arranged for him to see. On Collins's desk was a photograph of quite a different sort—a portrait of a very pretty girl whom Dirk thought he had seen once or twice at lunch. Collins must have noticed his interest, but as he didn't elucidate Dirk guessed that he was

still unmarried and, like himself, an optimistic bache-
lor.

"I suppose," the aerodynamicist said presently,
"you've seen our film, 'The Road to Space'?"

"Yes, I thought it was very good."

"It saves a lot of talking and puts over the basic
ideas pretty clearly. But of course it's rather out-of-
date now, and I guess you're still very much in the
dark about the latest developments—particularly the
atomic drive in the 'Prometheus.'"

"That's true," said Dirk. "It's a complete mystery
to me."

Collins gave a puzzled little grin.

"That baffles us," he complained. "From the technical point of view, it's far simpler than the internal
combustion engine which everyone understands perfectly. But for some reason, people assume that an
atomic drive *must* be incomprehensible, so they won't
even make an effort to understand it."

"I'll make the effort," Dirk laughed. "It's up to you
to do the rest. But please remember—I want to know
only just enough to follow what's happening. I've no
intention of setting myself up as a designer of spaceships!"

3

"I suppose I can assume," said Collins, a little doubt-
fully, "that you're quite happy about common-or-
garden rockets and understand how they work in a
vaccum?"

"I can see," replied Dirk, "that if you throw a lot
of matter away from you at great speed, there's bound
to be a recoil."

"Good. It's amazing how many people still seem to
think that a rocket has to have 'something to push
against,' as they invariably put it. You'll appreciate,
then, that a rocket designer is always trying to get the

maximum possible velocity—and a bit more—from the jet which drives his machine forward. Obviously, the speed of the exhaust determines the velocity which his rocket will attain.

"The old chemical rockets, like V.2, had jet speeds of one or two miles a second. With such performances, to carry a load of one ton to the Moon and back would have needed several *thousand* tons of fuel, which wasn't practicable. What everyone wanted was a weightless fuel supply. Atomic reactions, which are a million or more times as powerful as chemical ones, virtually gave us this. The energy released by the few pounds of matter in the first atomic bombs could have taken a thousand tons to the Moon—and back.

"But though the energy had been released, no one knew exactly how to use it for propulsion. That little problem has only just been solved, and it's taken thirty years to produce the very inefficient atomic rockets we have today.

"Look at the problem from this point of view. In the chemical rocket, we get our driving exhaust by burning a fuel and letting the hot gases acquire speed by expanding through a nozzle. In other words, we exchange heat for velocity—the hotter our combustion chamber, the faster the jet will leave it. We'd get the same result if we didn't actually burn the fuel at all, but heated the combustion chamber from some outside source. In other words, we could make a rocket by pumping any gas we liked—even air—into a heating unit, and then letting it expand through a nozzle. O.K.?"

"Yes, that's straightforward enough so far."

"Very well. Now as you know, you can get as much heat as you like out of an atomic pile by making it of richer and richer materials. If you overdo it, of course, the pile will melt down into a puddle of liquid uranium with carbon bobbing about on the surface. Long before that sort of thing happened, any sensible man would have got hull-down over the horizon."

"You mean it might go up like an atomic bomb?"

"No, it couldn't do that. But an unapproachable radioactive furnace could be just as nasty in its quiet way. However, don't look so alarmed—this couldn't happen if the most elementary precautions were taken.

"We had, then, to design some kind of atomic reactor which would heat a gas stream to a very high temperature indeed—at least 4,000 degrees Centigrade. Since all known metals melt a long way below this, the problem gave us a bit of a headache!

"The answer we produced is called the 'line-focused reactor.' It's a long, thin, plutonium pile, and gas is pumped in at one end and becomes heated as it travels through. The final result is a central core of intensely hot gas into which we can concentrate or focus the heat from the surrounding elements. In the middle the jet temperature is over 6,000 degrees—hotter than the sun—but where it touches the walls it's only a quarter of this.

"So far, I haven't said *what* gas we're going to use. I think you'll realize that the lighter it is—strictly speaking, the lower its molecular weight—the faster it will be moving when it comes out of the jet. Since hydrogen is the lightest of all elements, it would be the ideal fuel, with helium a fairly good runner-up. I ought to explain, by the way, that we still use the word 'fuel,' even though we don't actually burn it but simply use it as a working fluid."

"That's one thing that had me puzzled," confessed Dirk. "The old chemical rockets carried their own oxygen tanks, and it's a bit disconcerting to find that the present machines don't do anything of the sort."

Collins laughed.

"We could even use helium as a 'fuel,' " he said, "though that won't burn at all—or indeed take part in any chemical reaction.

"Now although hydrogen's the ideal working fluid, as I called it, it's impossible stuff to carry round. In the liquid state it boils at a fantastically low temperature, and it's so light that a spaceship would have to have fuel tanks the size of gasometers. So we carry it combined with carbon in the form of liquid methane—CH_4—which isn't hard to handle and has a reasonable density. In the reactor it breaks down to carbon and hydrogen. The carbon's a bit of a nuisance, and tends to clog the works, but it can't be helped. Every so often we get rid of it by turning off the main jet and flushing out the motor with a draft of oxygen. It makes quite a pretty firework display.

"That, then, is the principle of the spaceship's motors. They give exhaust speeds three times that of any chemical rocket, but even so still have to carry a tremendous amount of fuel. And there are all sorts of other problems I've not mentioned: shielding the crew from the pile radiations was the worst.

" 'Alpha,' the upper component of the 'Prometheus,' weighs about three hundred tons of which two hundred and forty are fuel. If it starts from an orbit around the Earth, it can just make the landing on the Moon and return with a small reserve.

"It has, as you know, to be carried up to that orbit by 'Beta.' 'Beta' is a very heavy, super-high-speed flying-wing, also powered by atomic jets. She starts as a ramjet, using air as 'fuel,' and only switches over to her methane tanks when she leaves the top of the atmosphere. As you'll realize, not having to carry any fuel for the first stage of the journey helps things enormously.

"At take-off, the 'Prometheus' weighs five hundred tons, and is not only the fastest but the heaviest of all flying machines. To get it airborne, Westinghouse have built us a five-mile-long electric launching track out in the desert. It cost nearly as much as the ship itself, but of course it will be used over and over again.

"To sum up, then: we launch the two components together and they climb until the air's too thin to operate the ramjets any more. 'Beta' then switches over to her fuel tanks and reaches circular velocity at a height of about three hundred miles. 'Alpha,' of course, hasn't used any fuel at all—in fact, its tanks are almost empty when 'Beta' carries it up.

"Once the 'Prometheus' has homed on the fuel containers we've got circling up there, the two ships separate, 'Alpha' couples up to the tanks with pipelines and pumps the fuel aboard. We've already practiced this sort of thing and know it can be done. Orbital refuelling, it's called, and it's really the key to the whole problem, because it lets us do the job in several stages. It would be quite impossible to build one huge spaceship that would make the journey to the Moon and back on a single load of fuel.

"Once 'Alpha's' tanked up, it runs its motors until it's built up the extra two miles a second to get out of its orbit and go to the Moon. It reaches the Moon after four days, stays there a week and then returns, getting back into the same orbit as before. The crew transfers to 'Beta,' which is still patiently circling with her very bored pilot (who won't get any of the publicity) and is brought down to Earth again. And that's all there is to it. What could be simpler?"

"You make me wonder," laughed Dirk, "why it hasn't been done years ago."

"That's the usual reaction," said Collins in mock disgust. "It's not easy for outsiders to realize the terrific problems that had to be overcome in almost every stage of the work. That's where the time and money went. It wouldn't have been possible, even now, without the world-wide research that's been going on for the last thirty years. Most of our job was collecting the results of other people's work and adapting them to our use."

"How much," said Dirk thoughtfully, "would you say the 'Prometheus' cost?"

"It's almost impossible to say. The research of the world's laboratories for two generations, right back to the 1929's, has gone into the machine. You should include the two billion dollars the atomic bomb project cost, the hundreds of millions of marks the Germans put into Peenemünde, and the scores of millions of pounds the British government spent on the Australian range."

"I agree, but you must have some idea of the money that actually went into the 'Prometheus' itself."

"Well, even there we got quite priceless technical assistance—and equipment—for nothing. However, Professor Maxton once calculated that the ships cost about ten million pounds in research and five million in direct construction. That means, someone pointed out, that we're buying the Moon for a pound a square mile! It doesn't seem a lot, and of course the later ships will be a good deal cheaper. Incidentally, I believe we're almost recovering our expenses for the first trip on the film and radio rights! But who cares about the money, anyway?"

His eyes wandered toward that photograph of the distant Earth, and his voice became suddenly thoughtful.

"We're gaining the freedom of the whole Universe, and all that that implies. I don't think it can be valued in terms of pounds and dollars. In the long run, knowledge always pays for itself in hard cash—but it's still absolutely beyond price."

4

Dirk's meeting with Professor Maxton and Raymond Collins marked an unconscious turning point in his thinking, and indeed in his way of life. He felt, perhaps wrongly, that he had now found the source of the ideas which McAndrews and Matthews had passed on to him at second-hand.

No one could have been more unlike the coldly passionless scientist of fiction than the Deputy Director-General. He was not only a first-class engineer, but he was obviously fully aware of the implications of his work. It would be a fascinating study to discover the motives which had led him, and his colleagues, into this field. The quest for personal power did not seem a likely explanation in the cases that Dirk had met. He must guard against wishful thinking, but these men seemed to have a disinterested outlook which was very refreshing. Interplanetary was inspired by a missionary zeal which technical competence and a sense of humor had preserved from fanaticism.

Dirk was still only partly aware of the effects his new surroundings were having on his own character. He was losing much of his diffidence; the thought of meeting strangers, which not long ago had filled him with mild apprehension or at least with annoyance, no longer worried him at all. For the first time in his life, he was with men who were shaping the future and not merely interpreting the dead past. Though he was only an onlooker, he was beginning to share their emotions and to feel with their triumphs and defeats.

"I'm quite impressed," he wrote in his Journal that evening, "by Professor Maxton and his staff. They seem to have a much clearer and wider view of Interplanetary's aims than the non-technical people I've met. Matthews, for instance, is always talking about the scientific advances which will come when we reach the Moon. Perhaps because they take that sort of thing for granted, the scientists themselves seem more interested in the cultural and philosophical repercussions. But I mustn't generalize from a few cases which may not be typical.

"I feel that I've now a pretty clear view of the whole organization. It's now mostly a matter of filling in details, and I should be able to do that from my notes and the mass of photostats I've collected. I no longer have the impression of being a stranger watching some incomprehensible machine at work. In fact, I now feel that I'm almost a part of the organization—though I mustn't let myself get too involved. It's impossible to be neutral, but *some* detachment is necessary.

"Until now I've had various doubts and reservations concerning space flight. I felt, subconsciously, that it was too big a thing for man. Like Pascal, I was terrified by the silence and emptiness of infinite space. I see now that I was wrong.

"The mistake I made was the old one of clinging to the past. Today I met men who think as naturally in millions of miles as I do in thousands. Once there was a time when a thousand miles was a distance beyond all comprehension, yet now it is the space we cover between one meal and the next. That change of scale is about to occur again—and with unprecedented swiftness.

"The planets, I see now, are no further away than our minds will make them. It will take the 'Prometheus' a hundred hours to reach the Moon, and all the time she will be speaking to Earth and the eyes of the world will be upon her. How little a thing interplanetary travel seems if we match it against the weeks and the months and the years of the great voyages of the past!

"Everything is relative, and the time will surely come when our minds embrace the Solar System as now they do the Earth. Then, I suppose, when the scientists are looking thoughtfully toward the stars, many will cry: 'We don't want interstellar flight! The nine planets were good enough for our grandfathers and they're good enough for us!'"

Dirk laid his pen down with a smile and let his mind wander in the realms of fantasy. Would Man ever face that stupendous challenge and send his ships into the gulf between the stars? He remembered a phrase he had once read: "Interplanetary distances are a million times as great as those to which we are accustomed in everyday life, but interstellar distances are a million-fold greater still." His mind quailed before the thought, but still he clung to that phrase: "Everything is relative." In a few thousand years, Man had come from coracle to spaceship. What might he yet do in the eons that lay ahead?

5

It would be false to suggest that the five men on whom the eyes of the world were now fixed regarded themselves as daring adventurers about to risk their lives in a stupendous scientific gamble. They were all practical, hard-headed technicians who had no intention of taking part in a gamble of any kind—at least, where their lives were concerned. There was a risk, of course, but one took risks when one caught the 8.10 to the City.

Each reacted in his own way to the publicity of the past week. They had expected it, and they had been well prepared. Hassell and Leduc had been in the public eye before and knew how to enjoy the experience while avoiding its more annoying aspects. The other three members of the crew, having fame thrust suddenly upon them, showed a tendency to huddle together for mutual protection. This move was fatal, as it made them easy meat for reporters.

Clinton and Taine were still sufficiently unused to the experience of being interviewed to enjoy it, but their Canadian colleague Jimmy Richards hated it. His replies, none too helpful at the beginning, became progressively more and more brusque as time went by and he grew tired of answering the same questions *ad nauseam*. On one famous occasion, when harried by a particularly overbearing lady reporter, his behavior became somewhat less than gallant. According to the description later circulated by Leduc, the interview went something like this:

"Good morning, Mr. Richards. I wonder if you'd mind answering a few questions for the *West Kensington Clarion?*"

Richards (bored but still fairly affable): "Certainly, though I have to meet my wife in a few minutes."

"Have you been married long?"

"About twelve years."

"Oh: any children?"

"Two: both girls, if I remember correctly."

"Does your wife approve of your flying off from Earth like this?"

"She'd better."

(Pause, during which interviewer realizes that, for once, her ignorance of shorthand is going to be no handicap.)

"I suppose you have always felt an urge to go out to the stars, to—er—place the flag of humanity upon other worlds?"

"Nope. Never thought about it until a couple of years ago."

"Then how did you get chosen for this flight?"

"Because I'm the second best atomic engineer in the world."

"The first being?"

"Professor Maxton, who's too valuable to risk."

"Are you at all nervous?"

"Oh, yes. I'm frightened of spiders, lumps of plutonium more than a foot across, and anything that makes noises in the night."

"I mean—are you nervous about this voyage?"

"I'm scared stiff. Look—you can see me trembling." (Demonstrates. Minor damage to furniture.)

"What do you expect to find on the Moon?"

"Lots of lava, and very little else."

(Interviewer wearing a hunted look, and now clearly preparing to disengage.)

"Do you expect to find any life on the Moon?"

"Very likely. As soon as we land, I expect there'll be a knock on the door and a voice will say: 'Would you mind answering a few questions for the *Selenites' Weekly?*'"

Not all interviews, of course, were anything like this flagrant example, and it is only fair to say that Richards swore the whole thing had been concocted by Leduc. Most of the reporters who covered Interplanetary's affairs were science graduates who had migrated into journalism. Theirs was a somewhat thankless task, since the newspaper world frequently regarded them as interlopers while the scientists looked upon them as apostates and backsliders.

Perhaps no single point had attracted more public interest than the fact that two of the crew would be reserves and would be fated to remain on Earth. For a time speculation about the ten possible combinations became so popular that the bookmakers began to take an interest in the subject. It was generally assumed that since Hassell and Leduc were both rocket pilots one but not both of them would be chosen. As this sort of discussion might have bad effects on the men themselves, the Director-General made it clear that no such argument was valid. Because of their training, *any* three men would form an efficient crew. He hinted, without making a definite promise, that the final choice might have to be made by ballot. No one, least of all the five men concerned, really believed this.

Hassell's preoccupation with his unborn son had now become common knowledge—which did not help matters. It had begun as a faint worry at the back of his mind which for a long time he had been able to keep under control. But as the weeks passed, it had come to trouble him more and more until his efficiency began to fall. When he realized this, it worried him still more and so the process had gathered momentum.

Since his fear was not a personal one, but concerned someone he loved, and since it had a logical foundation, there was little that psychologists could do about it. They could not suggest, to a man of his temperament and character, that he ask to be withdrawn from the expedition. They could only watch: and Hassell knew perfectly well that they were watching.

6

Dirk spent little time at Southbank during the days before the Exodus. It was impossible to work there: those who were going to Australia were too busy packing and tidying up their affairs, while those who weren't seemed in a very unco-operative mood. The irrepressible Matthews had been one of the sacrifices: McAndrews was leaving him in charge. It was a very sensible arrangement, but the two men were no longer on speaking terms. Dirk was very glad to keep out of their way, especially as they had been a little upset over his desertion to the scientists.

He saw equally little of Maxton and Collins, as the technical department was in a state of organized uproar. It had apparently been decided that *everything* might be needed in Australia. Only Sir Robert Derwent seemed perfectly happy amid the disorder, and Dirk was somewhat astonished to receive a summons from him one morning. As it happened, it came on one of the few days when he was at Headquarters. It was his first meeting with the Director-General since their brief introduction on the day of his arrival.

He entered somewhat timidly, thinking of all the tales he had heard about Sir Robert. The D.-G. probably noticed and understood his diffidence, for there was a distant twinkle in his eye as he shook hands and offered his visitor a seat.

The room was no larger than many other offices which Dirk had seen at Southbank, but its position at a corner of the building gave it an unrivaled view. One could see most of the Embankment from Charing Cross to London Bridge.

Sir Robert lost no time in getting to the point.

"Professor Maxton's been telling me about your job," he said. "I suppose you've got us all fluttering around in your killing-bottle, ready to be pinned down for posterity to examine?"

"I hope, Sir Robert," smiled Dirk, "that the final result won't be quite as static as that. I'm not here primarily as a recorder of facts, but of influences and motives."

The Director-General tapped thoughtfully on his desk, then remarked quietly: "And what motives, would you say, underlie our work?"

The question, through its very directness, took Dirk somewhat aback.

"They're very complex," he began defensively. "Provisionally, I'd say they fall into two classes—material and spiritual."

"I find it rather difficult," said the D.-G. mildly, "to picture a third category."

Dirk gave a slightly embarrassed smile.

"Perhaps I'm a little too comprehensive," he said. "What I mean is this: The first men seriously to advance the idea of interplanetary travel were visionaries in love with a dream. The fact that they were also technicians doesn't matter—they were, essentially, artists using their science to create something new. If space flight had been of no conceivable practical use, they would have wished to have achieved it just the same.

"Theirs was the spiritual motive, as I've called it. Perhaps 'intellectual' is a better word. You can't analyze it any further, because it represents a basic human impulse—that of curiosity. On the material side, you now have the vision of great new industries and engineering processes, and the desire of the billion-dollar communication companies to replace their myriads of surface transmitters by two or three stations out in space. This is the Wall Street side of the picture, which of course came a good deal later."

"And which motive," said Sir Robert, pressing on ruthlessly, "would you say is predominant here?"

Dirk was now beginning to feel completely at ease.

"Before I came to Southbank," he said, "I thought of Interplanetary—when I thought of it at all—as a group of technicians out for scientific dividends. That's what you pretend to be, and you deceive a lot of people. The description may apply to some of the middle grades of your organization—but it isn't true at the top."

Dirk drew back his bow, and took a long shot at that invisible target out there in the dark.

"I think that Interplanetary is run—and always has been run—by visionaries, poets if you like, who also happen to be scientists. Sometimes the disguise isn't very good."

There was silence for a while. Then Sir Robert said, in a somewhat subdued voice, though with a trace of a chuckle:

"It's an accusation that's been thrown at us before. We've never denied it. Someone once said that all human activity was a form of play. We're not ashamed of wanting to play with spaceships."

"And in the course of your play," said Dirk, "you will change the world, and perhaps the Universe."

He looked at Sir Robert with new understanding. He no longer saw that determined, bull-dog head with its broad sweep of brow, for he had suddenly remembered Newton's description of himself as a small child picking up brightly colored pebbles on the shore of the ocean of knowledge.

Sir Robert Derwent, like all great scientists, was such a child. Dirk believed that, in the final analysis, he would have crossed space for no other reason than to watch the Earth turning from night to day above the glittering lunar peaks, or to see Saturn's rings, in all their unimaginable glory, bridging the sky of his nearest moon.

7

The knowledge that this was his last day in London filled Dirk with a sense of guilty regret. Regret, because he had seen practically nothing of the place; guilt, because he couldn't help feeling that this was partly his own fault. It was true that he had been furiously busy, but looking back on the past few weeks it was hard to believe that he'd found it impossible to visit the British Museum more than twice, or St. Paul's Cathedral even once. He did not know when he would see London again, for he would return direct to America.

It was a fair but rather cool day, with the usual possibility of rain later. There was no work he could do at his flat, for all his papers had been packed and even now were halfway round the world ahead of him. He had said good-bye to those members of Interplanetary's staff he would not see again: most of the others he would meet at London Airport early tomorrow morning. Matthews, who seemed to have grown quite attached to him, had become almost tearful, and even his sparring partners Sam and Bert had insisted on a little farewell celebration at the office. When he walked away from Southbank for the last time, Dirk realized with a pang that he was also saying good-bye to one of the happiest periods of his life. It had been happy because it had been full, because it had extended all his resources to the utmost—above all, because he had been among men whose lives had a purpose which they knew was greater than themselves.

Meanwhile, he had an empty day on his hands and did not know how to occupy it. In theory, such a situation was impossible; but it seemed to have happened now.

He went into the quiet square, wondering if he had been wise to leave his raincoat behind. It was only a few hundred yards to the Embassy, where he had a little business to conduct, but he was rash enough to take a short cut. As a result he promptly lost himself in the labyrinth of side streets and culs-de-sac which made London such a continual source of exasperating delight. Only a lucky glimpse of the Roosevelt Memorial finally gave him his bearings again.

A leisurely lunch with some of his Embassy acquaintance at their favorite club disposed of the earlier afternoon; then he was left to his own resources. He could go anywhere he pleased, could see the places which otherwise he might always be sorry to have missed. Yet a kind of restless lethargy made him feel unable to do anything but wander at random through the streets. The sun had finally secured its bridgehead, and the afternoon was warm and relaxing. It was pleasant to drift through the back streets and to come by chance upon buildings older than the United States— yet bearing such notices as: "Grosvenor Radio and Electronic Corporation," or "Provincial Airways, Ltd."

Late in the afternoon Dirk emerged into what, he concluded, must be Hyde Park. For a full hour he circulated under the trees, always keeping within sight of the adjoining roads. The Albert Memorial held him paralyzed with frank disbelief for many minutes, but he finally escaped from its hypnotic spell and decided to cut back across the Park to Marble Arch.

He had forgotten the impassioned oratory for which that spot was famous, and it was very entertaining to wander from one crowd to another, listening to the speakers and their critics. What, he wondered, had ever given people the idea that the British were reserved and undemonstrative?

He stood for some time enthralled by a duet between one orator and his heckler in which each maintained with equal passion that Karl Marx had—and had *not*—made a certain remark. What the remark was Dirk never discovered, and he began to suspect that the disputants themselves had long since forgotten it. From time to time helpful interjections were provided by the good-natured crowd, which obviously had no strong feelings on the subject but wanted to keep the pot boiling.

The next speaker was engaged in proving, apparently with the aid of Biblical texts, that Doomsday was at hand. He reminded Dirk of those apocalyptic prophets of the anxious year A.D. 999; would their successors, ten centuries later, still be predicting the Day of Wrath as the year 1999 drew to its close? He could hardly doubt it. In many ways human nature changed very little: the prophets would still be there, and there would still be some to believe them.

He moved on to the next group. A small but attentive audience was gathered around an elderly, white-haired man who was giving a lecture—a remarkably well-informed lecture—on philosophy. Not all the speakers, Dirk decided, were by any means cranks. This lecturer might have been a retired schoolmaster with such strong views on adult education that he felt himself impelled to hold forth in the marketplace to all who would listen.

His discourse was on Life, its origin and its destiny. His thoughts, like those of his listeners, were no doubt influenced by that winged thunderbolt lying in the desert on the far side of the world, for presently he began to speak of the astronomical stage upon which the strange drama of life was being played.

He painted a vivid picture of the sun and its circling planets, taking the thoughts of his listeners with him from world to world. He had a gift for picturesque phrases, and though Dirk was not sure that he confined himself to accepted scientific knowledge, the general impression he gave was accurate enough.

Tiny Mercury, blistering beneath its enormous sun, he pictured as a world of burning rocks washed by sluggish oceans of molten metal. Venus, Earth's sister planet, was forever hidden from us by those rolling clouds which had not parted once during the centuries in which men had gazed upon her. Beneath that blanket might be oceans and forests and the hum of strange life. Or there might be nothing but a barren wilderness swept by scorching winds.

He spoke of Mars; and one could see a ripple of increased attention spread through his audience. Forty million miles outward from the Sun, Nature had scored her second hit. Here again was life: we could see the changing colors which on our own world spoke of the passing seasons. Though Mars had little water, and his atmosphere was stratospherically thin, vegetation and perhaps animal life could exist there. Of intelligence, there was no conclusive evidence at all.

Beyond Mars the giant outer worlds lay in a frozen twilight which grew ever dimmer and colder as the Sun dwindled to a distant star. Jupiters and Saturn were crushed beneath atmospheres thousands of miles deep—atmospheres of methane and ammonia, torn by hurricanes which we could observe across half a billion miles or more of space. If there was life on those strange outer planets, and the still colder worlds beyond, it would be more weird than anything we could imagine. Only in the temperate zone of the Solar System, the narrow belt in which floated Venus, Earth and Mars, could there be life as we knew it.

Life as we knew it! And how little we knew! What right had *we* on our puny world to assume that it set the pattern for all the Universe? Could conceit go farther?

The Universe was not hostile to life, but merely indifferent. Its strangeness was an opportunity and a challenge—a challenge which intelligence would accept. Shaw had spoken the truth, half a century ago, when he put these words into the mouth of Lilith, who came before Adam and Eve:

"Of Life only there is no end; and though of its million starry mansions many are empty and many still unbuilt, and though its vast domain is as yet unbearably desert, my seed shall one day fill it and master it to its uttermost confines."

The clear, cultured voice died away, and Dirk became once more conscious of his surroundings. It had been a remarkable performance: he would like to know more about the speaker, who was now quietly dismantling his little platform and preparing to wheel it away in a dilapidated handcart. The crowd was dispersing around him, looking for fresh attractions. From time to time half-heard phrases borne down the wind told Dirk that the other speakers were still operating at full blast.

Dirk turned to leave, and as he did so caught sight of a face which he recognized. For a moment he was taken completely by surprise: the coincidence seemed too improbable to be true.

Standing in the crowd, only a few feet away from him, was Victor Hassell.

8

Maude Hassell had needed no elaborate explanations when her husband had said, rather abruptly, that he was "going for a stroll around the Park." She understood perfectly, and merely expressed a hope that he wouldn't be recognized, and would be back in time for tea. Both of these wishes were doomed to disappointment, as she was fairly sure they would be.

Victor Hassell had lived in London for almost half his life, but his earliest impressions of the city were still the most vivid and still held the strongest place in his affections. As a young engineering student he had lodged in the Paddington area and had walked to college every day across Hyde Park and Kensington Gardens. When he thought of London, he did not picture busy streets and world-famous buildings, but quiet avenues of trees and open fields, and the wide sands of Rotten Row along which the Sunday morning riders would still be cantering on their fine horses when humanity's first ships were turning homeward from the stars. And there was no need for him to remind Maude of their first encounter beside the Serpentine, only two years ago, but a lifetime away. From all these places he must now take his leave.

He spent a little time in South Kensington, wandering past the old colleges which formed so large a part of his memories. They had not changed: the students with their folders and T-squares and slide-rules were just the same. It was strange to think that almost a century ago the young H. G. Wells had been one of that eager, restless throng.

Acting upon impulse, Hassell walked into the Science Museum and came, as he had so often done before, to the replica of the Wright biplane. Thirty years earlier the original machine had been hanging here in the great gallery, but it had long since gone back to the United States and few now remembered Orville Wright's protracted battle with the Smithsonian Institution which had been the cause of its exile.

Seventy-five years—a long lifetime, no more—lay between the flimsy wooden framework that had skimmed a few yards across the ground at Kitty Hawk, and the great projectile that might soon be taking him to the Moon. And he did not doubt that in another lifetime, the "Prometheus" would look as quaint and as primitive as the little biplane suspended above his head.

Hassell came out into Exhibition Road to find the sun shining brightly. He might have stayed longer in the Science Museum, but a number of people had been staring at him a little too intently. His chances of remaining unrecognized were, he imagined, probably lower inside this building than almost anywhere on Earth.

He walked slowly across the Park along the paths he knew so well, pausing once or twice to admire views he might never see again. There was nothing morbid in his realization of this: indeed, he could appreciate with some detachment the increased intensity it gave to his emotions. Like most men, Victor Hassell was afraid of death; but there were occasions when it was a justifiable risk. That, at least, had been true when there was merely himself to consider. He only wished he could prove it was still true, but in that he had so far failed.

There was a bench not far from Marble Arch where he and Maude had often sat together in the days before their marriage. He had proposed to her here a good many times, and she had turned him down almost—but not quite—as frequently. He was glad to see that it was unoccupied at the moment, and he dropped into it with a little sigh of satisfaction.

His contentment was short-lived, for less than five minutes later he was joined by an elderly gentleman who settled himself down behind a pipe and the *Manchester Guardian*. (That anyone should wish to guard Manchester had always struck Hassell as baffling in the extreme.) He decided to move, after a sufficient interval, but before he could do this without obvious rudeness there was a further interruption. Two small boys who had been strolling along the pathway did a sudden turn to starboard and walked up to the bench. They looked at him steadily in the uninhibited way that small boys have, then the elder said accusingly: "Hey, Mister, are you Vic Hassell?"

Hassell gave them a critical examination. They were clearly brothers, and as unattractive a pair as one would meet in a day's march. He shuddered slightly as he realized what a hazardous business parenthood was.

In normal circumstances, Hassell would have carefully confessed to the charge, since he had not forgotten many of his own schoolboy enthusiasms. He would probably have done so even now had he been approached more politely, but these urchins appeared to be playing truant from Dr. Fagin's Academy for Young Delinquents.

He looked at them fixedly and said, in his best Mayfair *circa* 1920 voice, "It's half-pass three, and I *haven't* any change for a sixpence."

At this masterly *non sequitur* the younger boy

turned to his brother and said heatedly: "Garn, George—I told you he weren't!"

The other slowly strangled him by twisting his tie and continued as if nothing had happened.

"You're Vic Hassell, the rocket bloke."

"Do I look like Mr. Hassell?" said Mr. Hassell in tones of indignant surprise.

"Yes."

"That's odd—no one's ever told me so."

This statement might be misleading, but it was the literal truth. The two boys looked at him thoughtfully: Junior had now been granted the luxury of respiration. Suddenly George appealed to the *Manchester Guardian,* though there was now a welcome note of uncertainty in his voice.

"He's kidding us, Mister, ain't he?"

A pair of spectacles reared themselves over the paper, and stared at them owlishly. Then they focused on Hassell, who began to feel uncomfortable. There was a long, brooding silence.

Then the stranger tapped his paper and said severely: "There's a photo of Mr. Hassell in here. The nose is quite different. Now please go away."

The paper barricade was re-erected. Hassell looked into the distance, ignoring his inquisitors, who continued to stare disbelievingly at him for another minute. Finally, to his relief, they began to move away, still arguing with each other.

Hassell was wondering if he should thank his unknown supporter when the other folded his newspaper and removed his glasses.

"You know," he said, with a slight cough, "there *is* a striking resemblance."

Hassell gave a shrug. He wondered if he should own up, but decided not to do so.

"To tell the truth," he said, "it has caused me some annoyance before."

The stranger looked at him thoughtfully, though his eyes had a misty, faraway look.

"They're leaving for Australia tomorrow, aren't they?" he said rhetorically. "I suppose they've got a fifty-fifty chance of coming back from the Moon?"

"I should say it's a lot better than that."

"Still, it *is* a chance, and I suppose at this very moment young Hassell's wondering if he'll ever see London again. It would be interesting to know what he's doing—you could learn a lot about him from that."

"I guess you could," said Hassell, shifting uncomfortably in his seat and wondering how he could get away. The stranger, however, seemed in a talkative mood.

"There's an editorial here," he said, waving his crumpled paper, "all about the implications of space flight and the effect it's going to have on everyday life. That sort of thing's all very well, but when are we going to *settle down*? Eh?"

"I don't quite follow you," said Hassell, not altogether truthfully.

"There's room for everyone on this world, and if we run it properly we'll not find a better, even if we go gallivanting right around the Universe."

"Perhaps," said Hassell mildly, "we'll only appreciate Earth when we have done just that."

"Humph! Then more fools us. Aren't we ever going to rest and have some peace?"

Hassell, who had met this argument before, gave a little smile.

"The dream of the Lotus Eaters," he said, "is a pleasant fantasy for the individual—but it would be death for the race."

Sir Robert Derwent had once made that remark and it had become one of Hassell's favorite quotations.

"The Lotus Eaters? Let's see—what did Tennyson say about them—nobody reads him nowadays. 'There is sweet music here that softer falls . . .' No, it isn't that bit. Ah, I have it!"

" 'Is there any peace
In ever climbing up the climbing wave?'

Well, young man, *is* there?"

"For some people—yes," said Hassell. "And per- haps when space flight arrives they'll all rush off to the planets and leave the Lotus Eaters to their dreams. That should satisfy everybody."

"And the meek shall inherit the Earth, eh?" said his companion, who seemed to have a very literary turn of mind.

"You could put it that way," smiled Hassell. He looked automatically at his watch, determined not to become involved in an argument which could have only one result.

"Dear me, I must be going. Thanks for the talk."

He rose to leave, thinking he'd preserved his in- cognito rather well. The stranger gave him a curious little smile and said quietly: "Good-bye." He waited until Hassell had gone twenty feet, then called after him in a louder voice: "And good luck—Ulysses!"

Hassell stopped dead, then swiveled round in his tracks—but the other was already walking briskly in the direction of Hyde Park Corner. He watched the tall, spare figure lose itself in the crowd; and only then did he say to himself explosively: "Well I'll be damned!"

Then he shrugged his shoulders and walked on towards Marble Arch, intending to listen once again to the soapbox orators who had given him so much amusement in his youth.

It did not take Dirk long to realize that the coin- cidence was hardly so surprising after all. Hassell, he remembered, lived in the West London area. What was more natural than that he, too, should be taking his last look at the city? It might well be his last in a far more final sense than Dirk's.

Their eyes met across the crowd. Hassell gave a little start of recognition, but Dirk did not suppose he would remember him by name. He pushed his way toward the young pilot and introduced himself somewhat awkwardly. Hassell would probably prefer to be left alone, but he could scarcely turn aside without speaking. Moreover, he had always wanted to meet the Englishman and this seemed far too good an opportunity to miss.

"Did you hear that last talk?" asked Dirk, by way of starting the conversation.

"Yes," replied Hassell. "I happened to be passing and overheard what the old chap was saying. I've often seen him here before; he's one of the saner specimens. It's rather a mixed bag, isn't it?" He laughed and waved in the general direction of the crowd.

"Very," said Dirk. "But I'm glad I've seen the place in action. It's quiet an experience."

As he spoke, he studied Hassell carefully. It was not easy to judge his age, which might have been anything from twenty-five to thirty-five. He was slightly built, with clearcut features and unruly brown hair. A scar from an early rocket crash ran diagonally across his left cheek, but was only visible now and then when the skin became taut.

"After listening to that talk," said Dirk, "I must say that the Universe doesn't sound a very attractive place. It's not surprising that a lot of people would prefer to stay at home."

Hassell laughed.

"It's funny you should say that; I've just been talking to an old fellow who was making the same point. He knew who I was, but pretended he didn't. The argument I brought forward was that there are two kinds of mind—the adventurous, inquisitive types and the stay-at-homes who're quite happy to sit in their own back-gardens. I think they're both necessary, and it's silly to pretend that one's right and the other isn't."

"I think I must be a hybrid," smiled Dirk. "I like to sit in my back-garden—but I also like the wanderers to drop in now and then to tell me what they've seen."

He broke off abruptly, then added: "What about sitting down for a drink somewhere?"

He felt tired and thirsty and so, for the same reason, did Hassell.

"Just for a moment, then," said Hassell. "I want to get back before five."

Dirk could understand this, though as it happened he knew nothing of the other's domestic preoccupations. He let Hassell navigate him to the lounge of the Cumberland, where they sat down thankfully behind a couple of large beers.

"I don't know," said Dirk with an apologetic cough, "if you've heard of my job."

"As a matter of fact I have," said Hassell with an engaging smile. "We were wondering when you were going to catch up with us. You're the expert on motives and influences, aren't you?"

Dirk was surprised, as well as a trifle embarrassed, to discover how far his fame had spread.

"Er—yes," he admitted. "Of course," he added hastily, "I'm not primarily concerned with individual cases, but it's very useful to me if I can find just how people got involved in astronautics in the first place."

He wondered if Hassell would take the bait. After a minute, he began to nibble and Dirk felt all the sensations of an angler watching his float twitching, at long last, on the surface of some placid lake.

"We're argued that often enough at the Nursery," said Hassell. "There's no simple answer. It depends on the individual."

Dirk generated an encouraging silence.

"Consider Taine, for example. He's the pure scientist, looking for knowledge and not much interested in the consequences. That's why, despite his brains, he'll always be a smaller man than the D.-G. Mind you—I'm not criticizing. One Sir Robert's probably quite enough for a single generation!

"Clinton and Richards are engineers and love machinery for its own sake, though they're much more human than Taine. I guess you've heard how Jimmy deals with reporters he doesn't like—I thought so! Clinton's a queer sort of fellow and you never know exactly what's going on in his mind. In their cases, however, they were chosen for the job—they didn't go after it.

"Now, Pierre's just about as different from the rest as he could be. He's the kind who likes adventure for itself—that's why he became a rocket pilot. It was his big mistake, though he didn't realize it at the time. There's nothing adventurous about rocket flying: either it goes according to plan—or else, *Bang!*"

He brought his fist down on the table, checking it in the last fraction of an inch so that the glasses scarcely rattled. The unconscious precision of the movement filled Dirk with admiration. He could not, however, let Hassell's remarks go unchallenged.

"I seem to remember," Dirk said, "a little contretemps of yours which must have given you a certain amount of—er—excitement."

Hassell smiled disparagingly.

"That sort of thing happens once in a thousand times. On the remaining nine hundred and ninety-nine occasions, the pilot's simply there because he weighs less than the automatic machinery that could do the same job."

He paused, looking over Dirk's shoulder, and a slow smile came across his face.

"Fame has its compensations," he murmured. "One of them is approaching right now."

A hotel dignitary was wheeling a little trolley toward them, wheeling it with the air of a high-priest bringing a sacrifice to the altar. He stopped at their table, and produced a bottle which, if Dirk could judge from its cobwebbed exterior, was considerably older than he himself.

"With the compliments of the management, sir,"

said the official, bowing toward Hassell, who made appreciative noises but looked a little alarmed at the attention now being concentrated on him from all sides.

Dirk knew nothing of wines, but he did not see how any skill in that complicated art could have made the smooth liquid slide more voluptuously down his throat. It was such a discreet, such a well-bred wine that they had no hesitation in toasting themselves, then Interplanetary, and then the "Prometheus." Their appreciation so delighted the management that another bottle would have been forthcoming immediately, but Hassell gracefully refused and explained that he was already very late, which was perfectly true.

They parted in a high good humor on the steps of the Underground, feeling that the afternoon had come to a brilliant *finale*. Not until Hassell had gone did Dirk realize that the young pilot had said nothing, absolutely nothing, about himself. Was it modesty— of merely lack of time? He had been surprisingly willing to discuss his colleagues; it seemed almost as if he was anxious to divert attention from himself.

Dirk stood worrying over this for a moment: then, whistling a little tune, he began to walk slowly homeward along Oxford Street. Behind him, the sun was going down upon his last evening in England.

Part Three

For thirty years the world had been slowly growing used to the idea that, some day, men were going to reach the planets. The prophecies of the early pioneers of astronautics had come true so many times since the first rockets climbed through the stratosphere that few people disbelieved them now. That tiny crater near Aristarchus, and the television films of the other side of the Moon were achievements which could not be denied.

Yet there had been some who had deplored or even denounced them. To the man in the street, interplanetary flight was still a vast, somewhat terrifying possibility just below the horizon of everyday life. The general public, as yet, had no particular feelings about space flight except the vague realization that "Science" was going to bring it about in the indefinite future.

Two distinct types of mentality, however, had taken astronautics very seriously indeed, though for quite different reasons. The practically simultaneous impact of the long-range rocket and the atomic bomb upon the military mind had, in the 1950's, produced a crop of blood-curdling prophecies from the experts in mechanized murder. For some years there had been much talk of bases on the Moon or even—more appropriately—upon Mars. The United States Army's belated

discovery, at the end of the Second World War, of
Oberth's twenty-year-old plans for "space-stations"
had revived ideas which it was a gross understatement
to call "Wellsian."

In his classic book, Wege zur Raumschiffahrt,
Oberth had discussed the building of great "space-
mirrors" which could focus sunlight upon the Earth,
either for peaceful purposes or for the incineration of
enemy cities. Oberth himself never took this last idea
very seriously, and must have been surprised at its
solemn reception two decades later.

The fact that it would be very easy to bombard the
Earth from the Moon, and very difficult to attack the
Moon from the Earth, had made many uninhibited
military experts declare that, for the sake of peace,
their particular country must seize our satellite before
any war-mongering rival could reach it. Such arguments were common in the decade following the release of atomic energy, and were a typical by-product
of that era's political paranoia. They died, unlamented,
as the world slowly returned to sanity and order.

A second and perhaps more important body of opinion, while admitting that interplanetary travel was possible, opposed it on mystical or religious grounds. The
"theological opposition," as it was usually termed, believed that man would be disobeying some divine edict
if he ventured away from his world. In the phrase of
Interplanetary's earliest and most brilliant critic, the
Oxford don C. S. Lewis, astronomical distances were
"God's quarantine regulations." If man overcame
them, he would be guilty of something not far removed
from blasphemy.

Since these arguments were not founded on logic,
they were quite irrefutable. From time to time Interplanetary had issued counterblasts, pointing out that
the same objections might very well have been brought
against all explorers who had ever lived. The astronomical distances which twentieth-century man could
bridge in minutes with his radio waves were less of a
barrier than the great oceans must have seemed to his

Stone Age ancestors. No doubt in prehistoric times there were those who shook their heads and prophesied disaster when the young men of the tribe went in search of new lands in the terrifying, unknown world around them. Yet it was well that the search had been made before the glaciers came grinding down from the Pole.

One day the glaciers would return; and that was the least of the dooms that might descend upon the Earth before its course was run. Some of these could only be guessed, but one at least was almost certain in the ages ahead.

There comes a time in the life of every star when the delicate balance of its atomic furnaces must tilt, one way or the other. In the far future the descendants of Man might catch, from the safety of the outermost planets, a last glimpse of their birthplace as it sank into the fires of the detonating Sun.

One objection to space flight which these critics brought forward was, on the face of it, more convincing. Since Man, they argued, had caused so much misery upon his own world, could he be trusted to behave on others? Above all, would the miserable story of conquest and enslavement of one race by another be repeated again, endlessly and forever, as human culture spread from one world to the next?

Against this there could be no fully convincing answer: only a clash of rival faiths—the ancient conflict between pessimism and optimism, between those who believed in Man and those who did not. But the astronomers had made one contribution to the debate by pointing out the falseness of the historical analogy. Man, who had been civilized only for a millionth of the life of his planet, was not likely to encounter races on other worlds which would be primitive enough for him to exploit or enslave. Any ships from Earth which set out across space with thoughts of interplanetary empire might find themselves, at the end of their voyage, with no greater hopes of conquest than a fleet of *savage war-canoes drawing slowly into New York harbor.*

The announcement that the "Prometheus" might be launched within a few weeks had revived all these speculations and many more. Press and radio talked of little else, and for a while the astronomers made a profitable business of writing guardedly optimistic articles about the Solar System. A Gallup poll carried out in Great Britain during this period showed that 41 per cent of the public thought interplanetary travel was a good thing, 26 per cent were against it, and 33 per cent had not made up their minds. These figures —particularly the 33 per cent—caused some despondency at Southbank and resulted in many conferences in the Public Relations Department, which was now busier than it had ever been before.

Interplanetary's usual trickle of visitors had grown to a mighty flood bearing upon its bosom some very exotic characters. Matthews had evolved a standard procedure for dealing with most of these. The people who wanted to go on the first trip were offered a ride in the Medical Section's giant centrifuge, which could produce accelerations of ten gravities. Very few accepted this offer, and those who did, when they had recovered, were then passed to the Dynamics Department, where the mathematicians administered the coup de grâce by asking them unanswerable questions.

No one, however, had found an effective means of dealing with the genuine cranks—though they could sometimes be neutralized by a kind of mutual reaction. It was one of Matthews's unfulfilled ambitions to be visited simultaneously by a flat-earther and one of those still more eccentric people who are convinced that the world is on the inside of a hollow sphere. This would, he was sure, result in a highly entertaining debate.

Very little could be done about the psychic explorers (usually middle-aged spinsters) who were already perfectly well acquainted with the Solar System and all too anxious to impart their knowledge. Matthews had been optimistic enough to hope, now that the crossing of space was so close at hand, that they would not be so eager to have their ideas tested by reality. He was disappointed, and one unfortunate member of his staff was employed almost full time listening to these ladies give highly colored and mutually incompatible accounts of lunar affairs.

More serious and significant were the letters and comments in the great newspapers, many of which demanded official replies. A minor canon of the Church of England wrote a vigorous and much publicized letter to The London Times, denouncing Interplanetary and all its works. Sir Robert Derwent promptly went into action behind the scenes and, as he put it, "trumped the fellow with an archbishop." It was rumored that he had a cardinal and a rabbi in reserve if attacks came from other quarters.

No one was particularly surprised when a retired brigadier, who had apparently spend the last thirty years in suspended animation in the outskirts of Aldershop, wanted to know what steps were being taken to incorporate the Moon into the British Commonwealth. Simultaneously, a long-dormant major-general erupted in Atlanta and asked Congress to make the Moon the Fiftieth State. Similar demands were to be heard in almost every country in the world —with the possible exception of Switzerland and Luxembourg—while the international lawyers realized that a crisis—of which they had long been warned was now almost upon them.

At this moment Sir Robert Derwent issued the famous manifesto which had been prepared many years ago against this very day.

"Within a few weeks," the message ran, "we hope to launch the first spaceship from the Earth. We do not know whether we shall succeed, but the power to reach the planets is now almost within our grasp. This generation stands upon the brink of the ocean of space, preparing for the greatest adventure in all history.

"There are some whose minds are so rooted in the

*past that they believe the political thinking of our an-
cestors can still be applied when we reach other worlds.
They even talk of annexing the Moon in the name of
this or that nation, forgetting that the crossing of space
has required the united efforts of scientists from every
country in the world.*

*"There are no nationalities beyond the strato-
sphere: any worlds we may reach will be the common
heritage of all men—unless other forms of life have
already claimed them for their own.*

*"We, who have striven to place humanity upon the
road to the stars, make this solemn declaration, now
and for the future:*

"We will take no frontiers into space."

1

"I think it's hard lines on Alfred," remarked Dirk,
"having to stay behind now that the fun's beginning."

McAndrews gave a noncommittal grunt.

"We couldn't both go," he said. "Headquarters is
being decimated as it is. Too many people seem to
think this is just a good excuse for a holiday."

Dirk forebore from comment, though sorely
tempted. In any case, his own presence could not be
regarded as strictly necessary. He conjured up a last
sympathetic picture of poor Matthews, staring gloom-
ily over the sluggish Thames, and turned his mind
to happier things.

The Kentish coastline was still visible astern, for the
liner had not yet gained its full height or speed. There
was scarcely any sense of movement, but suddenly Dirk
had an indefinable feeling of change. Others must have
noticed it also for Leduc, who was sitting opposite,
nodded with satisfaction.

"The ramjets are starting to fire," he said. "They'll
be cutting the turbines now."

"That means," put in Hassell, "that we're doing over a thousand."

"Knots, miles or kilometers an hour, or rods, poles or perches per microsecond?" asked somebody.

"For heaven's sake," groaned one of the technicians, "don't start *that* argument again!"

"When do we arrive?" asked Dirk, who knew the answer perfectly well but was anxious to create a diversion.

"We touch down at Karachi in about six hours, get six hours' sleep, and should be in Australia twenty hours from now. Of course we have to add—or subtract —about half a day for time difference, but someone else can work that out."

"Bit of a come-down for you, Vic," Richards laughed at Hassell. "Thie last time you went round the world it took you ninety minutes!"

"One mustn't exaggerate," said Hassell. "I was way out, and it took a good hundred. Besides, it was a day and a half before I could get down again!"

"Speed's all very well," said Dirk philosophically, "but it gives one a false impression of the world. You get shot from one place to another in a few hours and forget that there's anything in between."

"I quite agree," put in Richards unexpectedly. "Travel quickly if you *must,* but otherwise you can't beat the good old sailing yacht. When I was a kid I spent most of my spare time cruising around the Great Lakes. Give me five miles an hour—or twenty-five thousand. I've no use for stage-coaches or aeroplanes or anything else in between."

The conversation then became technical, and degenerated into a wrangle over the relative merits of jets, athodyds and rockets. Someone pointed out that the airscrews could still be seen doing good work in the obscurer corners of China, but he was ruled out of order. After a few minutes of this, Dirk was glad when McAndrews challenged him to a game of chess on a miniature board.

He lost the first game over Southeastern Europe,

and fell asleep before completing the second—probably through the action of some defense mechanism, as McAndrews was much the better player. He woke up over Iran, just in time to land and go to sleep again. It was therefore not surprising that when Dirk reached the Timor Sea, and readjusted his watch for Australian time, he was not quite sure whether he should be awake or not.

His companions, who had synchronized their sleep more efficiently, were in better shape and began to crowd to the observation ports as they neared the end of their journey. They had been crossing barren desert, with occasional fetile areas, for almost two hours when Leduc, who had been map-reading, suddenly cried out: "There it is—over on the left!"

Dirk followed his pointing finger. For a moment he saw nothing; then he made out, many miles away, the buildings of a compact little town. To one side of it was an airstrip, and beyond that, an almost invisible black line that stretched across the desert. It seemed to be an unusually straight railroad; then Dirk saw that it led from nowhere to nowhere. It began in the desert and ended in the desert. It was the first five miles of the road that would lead his companions to the Moon.

A few minutes later the great launching track was beneath them, and with a thrill of recognition Dirk saw the winged bullet of the "Prometheus" glistening on the airfield beside it. Everyone became suddenly silent, staring down at the tiny silver dart which meant so much to them but which only a few had ever seen save in drawings and photographs. Then it was hidden by a block of low buildings as the liner banked and they came in to land.

"So this is Luna City!" remarked someone without enthusiasm. "It looks like a deserted gold-rush town."

"Maybe it is," said Leduc. "They used to have gold mines in these parts, didn't they?"

"Surely you know," said McAndrews pompously, "that Luna City was built by the British Government around 1950 as a rocket research base. Originally it had an aborigine name—something to do with spears or arrows, I believe."

"I wonder what the aborigines think of these goings-on? There are still some of them out in the hills, aren't there?"

"Yes," said Richards, "they've got a reservation a few hundred miles away, well off the line of fire. They probably think we're crazy, and I guess they're right."

The truck which had collected the party at the airstrip came to a halt before a large office building.

"Leave your kit aboard," instructed the driver. "This is where you get your hotel reservations."

No one was much amused at the jest. Accommodation at Luna City consisted largely of Army huts, some of which were almost thirty years old. The more modern buildings would certainly be occupied by the permanent residents, and the visitors were full of gloomy forebodings.

Luna City, as it had been called for the last five years, had never quite lost its original military flavor. It was laid out like an Army camp, and though energetic amateur gardeners had done their best to brighten it up, their efforts had only served to emphasize the general drabness and uniformity.

The normal population of the settlement was about three thousand, of whom the majority were scientists or technicians. In the next few days there would be an influx limited only by the accommodation—and perhaps not even by that. One newsreel company had already sent in a consignment of tents, and its personnel were making anxious inquiries about Luna City's weather.

To his relief, Dirk found that the room allocated to him, though small, was clean and comfortable. About a dozen members of the administrative staff also occupied the block, while across the way Collins and the other scientists from Southbank formed a second colony. The Cockneys, as they christened themselves, quickly enlivened the place by such notices

as "To the Underground" and "Line-up here for 25
bus."

The first day in Australia was, for the whole party,
entirely occupied by the mechanics of getting settled
and learning the geography of the "city." The little
town had one great point in its favor—it was compact
and the tall tower of the meteorological building
served as a good landmark. The airstrip was about
two miles away, and the head of the launching track
another mile beyond that. Although everyone was
eager to see the spaceship, the visit had to wait until
the second day. In any case Dirk was far too busy
during the first twelve hours frantically trying to lo-
cate his notes and records, which seemed to have gone
astray somewhere between Calcutta and Darwin. He
eventually found them at Technical Stores, which was
on the point of consigning the lot back to England
as they couldn't find his name on Interplanetary's establishment list.

At the end of the first exhausting day, Dirk
nevertheless still had enough energy to record his
impressions of the place.

"*Midnight.* Luna City, as Ray Collins put it, looks
like 'good fun'—though I guess the fun would wear
off after a month or so. The accommodation is quite
reasonable, though the furniture is rather scanty and
there's no running water in the block. I'll have to go
half a mile to get a shower, but this is hardly 'rough-
ing it!'"

"McA. and some of his people are in this building.
I'd rather have been with Collins's crowd across the
way, but I can't very well ask to be transferred.

"Luna City reminds me of the Air Force bases I've
seen in the war films. It has the same bleakly efficient
appearance, the same atmosphere of restless energy.
And like an air base, it exits for a machine—the
spaceship instead of the bomber.

"From my window I can see, a quarter of a mile
away, the dark shape of some office buildings which
look very incongruous here in the desert under these

strange, brilliant stars. A few windows are still lit up and one could imagine that the scientists are working feverishly against time to overcome some last-minute difficulty. But I happen to know that said scientists are making a devil of a noise in the next block, entertaining their friends. Probably the burner of midnight oil is some unfortunate accountant or storekeeper trying to balance his books.

"A long way off to the left, through a gap in the buildings, I can see a faint smear of light low down on the horizon. The 'Prometheus' is out there, lying under the floodlights. It's strange to think that she—or rather 'Beta'—has been up into space a dozen times or more on those fueling runs. Yet 'Beta' belongs to our planet, while 'Alpha,' which is still earthbound, will soon be up among the stars, never to touch the surface of this world again. We're all very eager to see the ship, and won't waste any time tomorrow in getting out to the launching site.

"*Later:* Ray hauled me out to meet his friends. I feel flattered, since I noticed McA. and Co. weren't invited. I can't remember the names of anyone I was introduced to, but it was good fun. And so to bed."

2

Even when first seen from ground level a mile away, the "Prometheus" was an impressive sight. She stood on her multiple undercarriage at the edge of the great concrete apron around the launcher, the scoops of her air-intakes gaping like hungry mouths. The smaller and lighter "Alpha" lay in its special cradle a few yards away, ready to be hoisted into position. Both machines were surrounded with cranes, tractors and various types of mobile equipment.

A rope barrier was slung round the site, and the

truck halted at the opening in the cordon, beneath a large notice which read:

WARNING-RADIOACTIVE AREA!

No unauthorized persons allowed past
this point.
Visitors wishing to examine the ship,
contact Ext. 47 (Pub. Rel. IIa).

THIS IS FOR YOUR PROTECTION!

Dirk looked a little nervously at Collins as they gave their identities and were waved past the barrier.

"I'm not sure I altogether like this," he said.

"Oh," replied Collins cheerfully, "there's no need to worry, as long as you keep near me. We won't go near any dangerous areas. And I always carry one of these."

He pulled a small rectangular box out of his coat pocket. It appeared to be made of plastic and had a tiny loudspeaker set into one side.

"What is it?"

"Geiger alarm. Goes off like a siren if there's any dangerous activity around."

Dirk waved his hand toward the great machine looming ahead of them.

"Is it a spaceship or an atomic bomb?" he asked plaintively.

Collins laughed.

"If you got in the way of the jet, you'd never notice the difference."

They were now standing beneath the slim, pointed snout of "Beta" and her great wings, sweeping away from them on either side, made her look like a moth in repose. The dark caverns of the air-scoops looked ominous and menacing, and Dirk was puzzled by the strange fluted objects which protruded from them at various places. Collins noticed his curiosity.

"Shock diffusers," he explained. "It's quite impossible to get one kind of air-intake to operate over the whole speed range from five hundred miles an hour at sea level to eighteen thousand miles an hour at the top of the stratosphere. Those gadgets are adjustable and can be moved in and out. Even so the whole thing's shockingly inefficient and only the fact that we've unlimited power makes it possible at all. Let's see if we can get aboard."

Her stubby undercarriage made it easy to enter the machine through the airlock door in her side. The rear of the ship, Dirk noticed, had been carefully fenced off with great movable barriers so that no one could approach it. He commented on this to Collins.

"That part of 'Beta,' " said the aerodynamicist grimly, "is Strictly Out of Bounds until the year 2000 or so."

Dirk looked at him blankly.

"What do you mean?"

"Just that. Once the atomic drive's started to operate, and the piles get radioactive, nothing can ever go near them again. They won't be safe to touch for years."

Even Dirk, who was certainly no engineer, began to realize the practical difficulties this must involve.

"Then how the devil do you inspect the motors, or put things right when they've gone wrong? Don't tell me that your designs are so perfect that there aren't any breakdowns!"

Collins smiled.

"That's the biggest headache of atomic engineering. You'll have a chance to see how it's done later."

There was surprisingly little to see aboard "Beta," since most of the ship consisted of fuel tanks and motors, invisible and unapproachable behind their barriers of shielding. The long, thin cabin at the nose might have been the control room of any airliner, but was more elaborately appointed since the crew of pilot and maintenance engineer would be living aboard her for nearly three weeks. They would have a very boring time, and Dirk was not surprised to see that the ship's equipment included a microfilm library and projector. It would be unfortunate, to say the least, if the two men had incompatible personalities: but no doubt the psychologists had checked this point with meticulous care.

Partly because he understood so little of what he saw, and partly because he was more anxious to go aboard "Alpha," Dirk soon grew tired of examining the control room. He walked to the tiny, thick windows and looked at the view ahead.

"Beta" was pointing out across the desert, almost parallel with the launching track over which she would be racing in a few days' time. It was easy to imagine that, even now, she was waiting to leap into the sky and to climb toward the stratosphere with her precious burden. . . .

The floor suddenly trembled as the ship began to move. Dirk felt a cold hand clutch at his heart and he almost overbalanced, only saving himself by grabbing at a rail in front of him. Not until then did he see the little tractor fussing around the ship and realize he had made a fool of himself. He hoped that Ray hadn't noticed his behavior, for he must certainly have turned pretty green.

"O.K.," said Collins at last, having finished his careful inspection. "Now let's look at 'Alpha.' "

They climbed out of the machine, which had now been pushed farther back into its surrounding barriers.

"I guess they're doing something to the motors," said Collins. "They've made—let's see—fifteen runs now without any trouble. Which is quite a feather in Prof. Maxton's cap."

Dirk was still wondering how "they" were doing anything at all to those terrifying inaccessible engines, but another query had crossed his mind.

"Listen," he said, "there's one thing I've been meaning to have out with you for some time. What sex *is* the 'Prometheus?' Everyone seems to use he, she or it quite impartially. I don't expect scientists to understand grammar, but still——"

Collins chuckled.

"That's just the kind of point we *are* particular about," he said. "It's been laid down officially somewhere. Although 'Prometheus' is, of course, 'he,' we call the entire ship 'she', as in nautical practice. 'Beta' is also 'she,' but 'Alpha,' the spaceship, is an 'it.' What could be simpler?"

"Quite a lot of things. However, I suppose it's O.K. as long as you're consistent. I'll jump on you when you aren't."

"Alpha" was an even more compact mass of motors and fuel tanks than the bigger ship. It had, of course, no fins or aerofoils of any kind, but there were signs that many oddly-shaped devices had been retracted into the hull. Dirk asked his friend about these.

"Those will be the radio antennae, periscopes, and outriggers for the steering jets," explained Collins. "Back at the rear you'll see where the big shock absorbers for the lunar landing have been retracted. When 'Alpha's' out in space they can all be extended and the crew can check 'em over to see if they're working properly. They can then stay out for good, since there's no air resistance for the rest of the voyage."

There was radiation screening around "Alpha's" rocket units, so it was impossible to get a complete view of the spaceship. It reminded Dirk of the fuselage of an old-fashioned airliner which had lost its wings or was yet to acquire them. In some ways "Alpha" strongly resembled a giant artillery shell, with an unexpected circlet of portholes near the nose. The cabin for the crew occupied less than a fifth of the rocket's length. Behind it were the multitudinous machines and controls which would be needed on the half-million-mile journey.

Collins roughly indicated the different sections of the machine.

"Just behind the cabin," he said, "we've put the

airlock and the main controls which may have to be adjusted in flight. Then come the fuel tanks—six of them—and the refrigeration plant to keep the methane liquid. Next we have the pumps and tur- bines, and then the motor itself whch extends halfway along the ship. There's a great wad of shielding around it, and the whole of the cabin is in the radi- ation shadow so that the crew gets the maximum protection. But the rest of the ship's 'hot,' though the fuel itself helps a good deal with the shielding."

The tiny airlock was just large enough to hold two people, and Collins went ahead to reconnoiter. He warned Dirk in advance that the cabin would prob- ably be too full to admit visitors, but a moment later he emerged again and signaled for him to enter.

"Everyone except Jimmy Richards and Digger Clin- ton had gone over to the workshops," he said. "We're in luck—there's bags of room."

That, Dirk soon discovered, was a remarkable exaggeration. The cabin had been designed for three people living under zero gravity, when walls and floor were freely interchangable and its whole volume could be used for any purpose. Now that the machine was lying horizontally on Earth, conditions were decidely cramped.

Clinton, the Australian electronics specialist, was half buried in a vast wiring diagram which he had been forced to wrap around himself in order to get it into the cabin. He looked, Dirk thought, rather like a caterpillar spinning its cocoon. Richards seemed to be running through some tests on the controls.

"Don't look alarmed," he said as Dirk watched him anxiously. "We won't take off—there's nothing in the fuel tanks!"

"I'm getting rather a complex about this," Dirk confessed. "Next time I come aboard, I'd like to make sure that we're tied down to a nice, fat anchor."

"As some anchors go," laughed Richards, "it needn't be such a big one. 'Alpha' hasn't much thrust

—about a hundred tons. But it can keep it up for a long time!"

"Only a hundred tons thrust? But she weighs three times that!"

Collins coughed delicately in the background.

"*It*, I thought we decided," he remarked. However, Richards seemed willing to adopt the new gender.

"Yes, but she's in free space when she starts, and when she takes off from the Moon her effective weight will be only about thirty-five tons. So everything's under control."

The layout of "Alpha's" cabin seemed to be the result of a pitched battle between science and surrealism. The design had been determined by the fact that for eight days the occupants would have no gravity at all, and would know nothing of "up" or "down"; while for a somewhat longer period, when the ship was standing on the Moon, there would be a low gravitational field along the axis of the machine. As at the moment the center-line was horizontal, Dirk had a feeling that he should really be walking on the walls or roof.

Yet it was a moment he would remember all his life, this visit to the first of all spaceships. The little portholes through which he was now looking would, in a few days' time, be staring out across the lonely lunar plains; the sky above would not be blue, but black and studded with stars. If he closed his eyes, he could almost imagine he was on the Moon already, and that if he looked through the upper portholes he would see the Earth hanging in the heavens. Though he went over the ship several times again, Dirk was never able to recapture the emotions of this first visit.

There was a sudden scrambling noise in the airlock and Collins said hastily:

"We'd better get out before the rush starts and someone gets trampled to death. The boys are coming back."

He managed to hold off the boarding party long enough for them to make good their escape. Dirk saw that Hassell, Leduc, Taine and three other men were all preparing to enter the ship—several with large pieces of equipment—and his mind boggled as he tried to picture conditions within. He hoped that nothing or nobody got broken.

Down on the concrete apron he relaxed and stretched himself again. He glanced up at one of the portholes to see what was happening in the ship, but was hardly surprised to find his view effectively blocked. Someone was sitting on the window.

"Well," said Collins, offering him a welcome cigarette. "What do you think of our little toys?"

"I can see where all the money's gone," Dirk answered. "It seems an awful lot of machinery to take three men just across the road, as you put it."

"There's some more to see yet. Let's go over to the launcher."

The launching track was impressive by its very simplicity. Two sets of rails began in the concrete apron —and went straight out to disappear over the horizon. It was the finest example of perspective that Dirk had ever seen.

The catapult shuttle was a huge metal carriage with arms that would grasp the "Prometheus" until the ship had gained flying speed. It would be just too bad, Dirk thought, if they failed to release at the right time.

"Launching five hundred tons at as many m.p.h. must take quite a generating plant," he said to Collins. "Why doesn't the 'Prometheus' take off under her own power?"

"Because with that initial loading she stalls at four-fifty, and the ramjets don't operate until just above that. So we have to get up speed first. The energy for the launch comes from the main power station over there; that smaller building beside it houses a battery of flywheels which are brought up to speed just before the take-off. Then they're coupled directly to the generators."

"I see," said Dirk. "You wind up the elastic, and away she goes."

"That's the idea," Collins replied. "When 'Alpha's' launched, 'Beta' isn't overloaded any more, and can be brought in to land at a reasonable speed—less than two hundred and fifty miles an hour; which is easy to anyone who makes a hobby of flying two-hundred-ton gliders!"

3

The milling crowd in the little hanger became suddenly quiet as the Director-General climbed up on to the dais. He had spurned amplifiers, and his voice rang strongly between the metal walls. As he spoke, hundreds of stylos began to race over hundreds of pads.

"I'd like," Sir Robert began, "to have a few words with you now that everyone's here. We're particularly anxious to assist you in your job, and to give you every opportunity of reporting the take-off, which as you know is in five days' time.

"First of all, you'll realize that it's physically impossible to let everyone look over the ship. We've admitted as many as we could in the last week, but after tomorrow we can accept no more visitors aboard. The engineers will be making their final adjustments then —and I might also say that we've already had one or two cases of—ahem!—souvenir hunting.

"You've all had a chance of selecting observation sites along the launching track. There should be plenty of room for everyone in the first four kilometers. But remember—*no one must go past the red barrier at five kilometers*. That's where the jets start firing, and it's still slightly radioactive from previous launchings. When the blast opens up, it will spray fission products over a wide area. We'll give the all-clear as soon as it's safe for you to collect the automatic cameras you have mounted out there.

"A number of people have asked when the radiation shields are being taken away from the ships so that they can be seen properly. We'll be doing this tomorrow afternoon and you can come and watch then. Bring binoculars or telescopes if you want to look at the jet units—you won't be allowed closer than a hundred yards. And if anyone thinks this is a lot of nonsense, there are two people in the hospital here who sneaked up to have a good look and now wish they hadn't.

"If for any reason there's a last-minute hold-up, launching will be delayed twelve hours, twenty-four hours, or, at the most, thirty-six hours. After that we'll have to wait for the next lunation—that is, for four weeks. It makes very little difference *when* we go to the Moon, as far as the ship is concerned, but we're anxious to land in daylight in the region we know best.

"The two components will separate about an hour after take-off. It should be possible to see 'Alpha's' blast if the rocket is above the horizon when it begins its powered orbit. We will be relaying any broadcast messages over the camp speaker system, and on our local wave-length.

" 'Alpha' should be on its way to the Moon, in free fall, about ninety minutes after take-off. We expect the first broadcast about then. After that, there will be nothing much happening for three days, when the braking maneuvers begin, about thirty thousand miles from the Moon. If for any reason the fuel consumption has been too high, there will be no landing. The ship will be turned into an orbit around the Moon, at a height of a few hundred kilometers, and will circle it until the time for the precomputed return flight.

"Now, are there any questions?"

There was silence for a minute. Then someone from the back of the crowd called out:

"When do you we know who's going to be in the crew, sir?"

The Director-General gave a worried little smile.

"Probably tomorrow. But please remember—this thing is much too big for personalities. It doesn't matter a damn *who* actually goes on the first flight. The journey itself is what counts."

"Can we talk to the crew when the ship's in space?"

"Yes, there will be limited opportunities for doing that. We hope to arrange a general broadcast once a day. And, of course, we'll be exchanging fixes and technical information continuously, so the ship will always be in contact with ground stations somewhere on Earth."

"What about the actual landing on the Moon—how's that being broadcast?"

"The crew will be much too busy to give running commentaries for our benefits. But the microphones will be live, so we'll have a good idea of what's happening. Also the observatories will be able to see the jet when it's firing. It will probably create quite a disturbance when it hits the Moon."

"What's the program after the landing, sir?"

"The crew will decide it in the light of circumstances. Before they leave the ship, they'll broadcast a description of everything they see, and the television camera will be set panning. So we should have some really good pictures—it's a full color system, by the way.

"That will take about an hour, and will give time for any dust and radiation products to disperse. Then two members of the crew will put on spacesuits and start exploring. They will radio back their impressions to the ship, and these will be relayed directly to Earth.

"We hope it will be possible to make a fair survey of a region about ten kilometers across, but we're taking no risks at all. Thanks to the television link, anything that's discovered can be shown immediately to us back on Earth. What we're particularly anxious to find, of course, are mineral deposits from which we can manufacture fuel on the Moon. We'll naturally be looking for signs of life as well, but no one will be more surprised than us if we find any."

"If you catch a Selenite," said someone facetiously, "will you bring him back for the zoo?"

"Certainly not!" said Sir Robert firmly, but with a twinkle in his eye. "If we start that sort of thing, we're likely to end up in zoos ourselves."

"When will the ship be coming back?" asked another voice.

"It will land in the early morning, and take off again in the late afternoon, lunar time. That means a stay of about eight of our days. The return trip lasts four and a half days, so the total absence will be sixteen to seventeen days.

"No more questions? Right, then I'll leave it at that. But there's one other thing. To make sure that everyone has a clear idea of the technical background, we've arranged three talks in the next few days. They'll be given by Taine, Richards and Clinton, and each will cover his special line of territory—but in nontechnical language. I strongly advise you not to miss them. Thank you!"

The ending of the address could not have been more perfectly timed. As the Director-General stepped down from the dais, a sudden, tremendous thunder came rolling up across the desert, setting the steel hangar reverberating like a drum.

Three miles away, "Alpha" was testing its motors at perhaps a tenth of their full power. It was a sound that tore at the ear drums and set the teeth on edge; what it would be like at full thrust was beyond imagination.

Beyond imagination, and beyond knowledge, for no one would ever hear it. When "Alpha's" rockets fired again, the ship would be in the eternal silence between the worlds, where the explosion of an atomic bomb is as soundless as the clash of snowflakes beneath a winter moon.

4

Professor Maxton looked rather tired as he arranged the maintenance sheets carefully on his desk in a neat pile. Everything had been checked; everything was working perfectly—almost too perfectly, it seemed.

The motors would have their final inspection tomorrow; meanwhile the stores could be moved into the two ships. It was a pity, he meditated, that one had to leave a stand-by crew aboard "Beta" while she circled the Earth. But it could not be avoided, since the instruments and the refrigeration plant for the fuel had to be looked after, and both machines would have to be fully maneuverable in order to make contact again. One school of thought considered that "Beta" should land and take off once more a fortnight later to meet the returning "Alpha." There had been much argument over this, but the orbital view had finally been accepted. It would be introducing fewer additional hazards to leave "Beta" where she was, already in position just outside the atmosphere.

The machines were ready; but what, thought Maxton, of the men? He wondered if the Director-General had yet made his decision, and abruptly decided to go to see him.

He was not surprised to find the chief psychologist already with Sir Robert. Dr. Groves gave him a friendly nod as he entered.

"Hello, Rupert. I suppose you're afraid I've called the whole thing off?"

"If you *did*," said Maxton grimly, "I think I'd get up a scratch crew from my staff and go myself. We'd probably manage pretty well, at that. But, seriously, how are the boys?"

"They're fine. It won't be easy to choose your three men—but I hope you can do it soon, as the waiting puts an unfair strain on them. There's no further reason for delay, is there?"

"No; they've all been reaction-tested on the controls and are fully familiar with the ship. We're all set to go."

"In that case," said the Director-General, "we'll settle it first thing tomorrow."

"How?"

"By ballot, as we promised. It's the only way to prevent bad feeling."

"I'm glad of that," said Maxton. He turned to the psychologist again.

"Are you *quite* sure about Hassell?"

"I was coming to him. He'll go all right, and he really wants to go. He's not worrying so much now that the last-minute excitement has got hold of him. But there's still one snag."

"What's that?"

"I think this is *very* unlikely, but suppose anything goes wrong at this end while he's on the Moon? The baby's due just around mid-voyage, you know."

"I see. If his wife died, to take the worst case, what effect would it have on him?"

"It isn't easy to answer that, as he'll already be under conditions quite unlike any which a human being has experienced before. He may take it calmly, or he may crack up. I think it's a vanishingly small risk, but it's there."

"We could, of course, lie to him," said Sir Robert thoughtfully, "but I've always been rather particular about ends and means. I'd hate to have a trick like that on my conscience."

There was silence for a few minutes. Then the Director-General continued:

"Well, thanks very much, Doctor. Rupert and I will talk it over. If we decide it's absolutely necessary, we might ask Hassell to step down."

The psychologist paused at the door.

"You *might*," he said, "but I'd hate to try it myself."

The night was ablaze with stars when Professor Maxton left the Director-General's office and walked wearily across to the living-quarters. It gave him a guilty feeling to realize that he didn't know the names of half the constellations he could see. One night he'd get Taine to identify them for him. But he would have to hurry; Taine might have only three more nights on Earth.

Over to the left he could see the crew's quarters,

blazing with lights. He hesitated for a moment, then walked swiftly toward the low building.

The first room, Leduc's, was empty, though the lights were on and it had only just been vacated. Its occupant had already stamped his personality upon it and piles of books lay around the place—far more than there seemed any point in bringing on such a short visit. Maxton glanced at the titles—mostly French—and once or twice his eyebrows rose slightly. He filed away one or two words to await his next contact with a really comprehensive French dictionary.

A charming photograph of Pierre's two children, sitting happily in a model rocket, was in a place of honor upon the desk. A portrait of his very beautiful wife was standing on the dressing-table, but the effect of domesticity was somewhat spoiled by the half-dozen photographs of other young ladies pinned on the wall.

Maxton moved to the next room, which happened to be Taine's. Here he found Leduc and the young astronomer deeply engrossed in a game of chess. He watched their tactics critically for a time, with the usual result that they accused him of ruining their play. At this he challenged the winner; Leduc won and Maxton polished him off in about thirty moves.

"That," he said, as the board was put away, "should stop you getting over-confident, Dr. Groves says it's a common failing of yours."

"Has Dr. Groves said anything else?" asked Leduc with elaborate casualness.

"Well, I'm giving away no medical confidences when I say that you've all passed your tests and can go on to High School. So first thing tomorrow we're going to have a sweepstake to select the three guinea pigs."

Expressions of relief came over his listeners' faces. They had been almost promised, it was true, that the final choice would be by ballot. But until now they had not been sure, and the feeling that they were all potential rivals had sometimes strained their relationships.

"Are the rest of the boys in?" asked Maxton. "I think I'll go and tell them."

"Jimmy's probably asleep," said Taine, "but Arnold and Vic are still awake."

"Good. Be seeing you in the morning."

Strange noises emerging from Richards' room showed that the Canadian was very much asleep. Maxton went on down the passage and knocked at Clinton's door.

The scene that confronted him almost took his breath away: it might have been a film set showing a mad scientist's laboratory. Lying on the floor in a tangle of radio tubes and wiring, Clinton seemed to be hypnotized by a cathode-ray oscilloscope, the screen of which was filled with fantastic geometrical figures, continually shifting and changing. In the background a radio was softly playing Rachmaninoff's rightly little-known Fourth Piano Concerto, and Maxton slowly realized that the figures on the screen were synchronized with the music.

He clambered on to the bed, which seemed the safest place to be, and watched until Clinton finally pried himself off the floor.

"Assuming that you know yourself," he said at last, "can you tell me what the heck you're trying to do?"

Clinton tiptoed gingerly over the confusion and sat down beside him.

"It's an idea I've been working on for some years," he explained apologetically.

"Well, I hope you remember what happened to the late Mr. Frankenstein."

Clinton, who was a serious individual, failed to respond.

"I call it a kaleidophone," he said. "The idea is that it will convert any rhythmical sound, such as music, into pleasing and symmetrical, but always changing, visual patterns."

"That would make an amusing toy. But would the average nursery run to that number of radio tubes?"

"It's *not* a toy," said Clinton, slightly hurt. "The television people, and the cartoon film industry, would find it very useful. It would be ideal for providing interludes during long musical broadcasts, which always get boring. In fact, I was hoping to make a bit of money out of it."

"My dear fellow," grinned Maxton, "if you're one of the first men to get to the Moon, I don't think you'll ever be in any real danger of starving in the gutter in your old age."

"No, I suppose not."

"The real reason why I stopped in was to tell you that we've having a ballot for the crew first thing to-morrow. Don't electrocute yourself before then. I'm going to see Hassell now—so good night."

Hassell was lying in bed reading when Professor Maxton knocked and entered.

"Hello, Prof," he said. "What are you doing around at this ungodly hour?"

Maxton came straight to the point.

"We're having the draw for the crew tomorrow morning. Thought you'd like to know."

Hassell was silent for a moment.

"That means," he said, in a slightly thick voice, "that we've all got through."

"Good heavens, Vic," protested Maxton heartily, "surely *you* never had any doubts!"

Hassell's eyes seemed to avoid him. They also avoided, Maxton noticed, the photograph of his wife on the dressing-table.

"As you all know," Hassell said presently, "I've been rather worried about—Maude."

"That's natural enough, but I gather that everything is O.K. What are you going to call the boy, by the way?"

"Victor William."

"Well, I guess that when he arrives Vic Junior will be about the most famous baby in the world. Too bad the television system's one-way. You'll have to wait until you get back before you can see him."

"When and if," muttered Hassell.

"Look here, Vic," said Maxton firmly. "You *do* want to go, don't you?"

Hassell looked up in half-ashamed defiance.

"Of course I do," he snapped.

"Very well then. You've got three chances in five of being chosen, like everyone else. But if you don't come out of the hat this time, then you'll be on the second trip, which in some ways will be even more important, since by then we'll be making our first attempt to establish a base. That's fair enough, isn't it?"

Hassell was silent for a moment. Then he said somewhat despondently:

"The first voyage will be the one that History will remember. After that, they'll all merge together."

Now was the moment, Professor Maxton decided, to lose his temper. He could do this with great skill and accuracy when the occasion demanded it.

"Listen to me, Vic," he stormed. "What about the people who *built* the blasted ship? How do you think *we* like having to wait until the tenth or the twentieth or the hundredth crossing before we have our chance? And if you're such a damn fool as to want fame— then good God, man, have you forgotten—*someone's got to pilot the first ship to Mars!*"

The explosion died away. Then Hassell grinned across at him and gave him a little laugh.

"Can I take that as a promise, Prof?"

"It isn't mine to make, confound you."

"No, I don't suppose it is. But I see your argument —if I miss the boat this time I won't be too upset. Now I think I'll go to sleep."

5

The spectacle of the Director-General carefully carrying a wastepaper basket into Professor Maxton's office might normally have caused some amusement, but everyone regarded him solemnly as he entered. There were no bowler hats, it seemed, in the whole of Luna

City: the wastepaper basket would have to act as a less dignified substitute.

Apart from the five members of the crew, who were painstakingly showing their nonchalance in the background, the only other people in the room were Maxton, McAndrews, two members of the administrative staff—and Alexson. Dirk had no particular reason to be there but McAndrews had invited him in. The Director of Public Relations was always doing helpful things like this, but Dirk strongly suspected that he was trying to secure his foothold in the official history.

Professor Maxton picked up a dozen small strips of paper from his desk and flicked them between his fingers.

"Right—are we all ready?" he said. "Here's a slip for each of you to put your name on. If anyone's too nervous to write, he can make a cross and we'll get it witnessed."

This little sally did much to relieve the tension and there were some good-natured jibes as the slips were signed and handed back, already folded.

"Good; now I'll mix them up with the blanks—so. Who'd like to do the draw?"

There was a moment's hesitation. Then, acting on some unanimous impulse, the four other crew members pushed Hassell to the front. He looked rather sheepish as Professor Maxton held the basket out toward him.

"No cheating, Vic!" he said. "And only one at a time! Close your eyes and dip."

Hassell plunged his hand into the basket and pulled out one of the slips. He handed it to Sir Robert, who quickly unfolded it.

"Blank," he said.

There was a little sigh of annoyance—or relief?

Another slip. Again—

"Blank."

"Hey, is everyone using invisible ink?" asked Maxton. "Try again, Vic."

This time he was lucky.

"P. Leduc."

Pierre said something very quickly in French and looked extremely pleased with himself. Everyone congratulated him hastily and turned at once back to Hassell.

He immediately scored a second bull's-eye.

"J. Richards."

Tension was now at its highest. Looking carefully, Dirk saw that Hassell's hand was trembling very slightly as he pulled out the fifth strip.

"Blank."

"Here we go again!" groaned someone. He was right.

"Blank."

And yet a third time—

"Blank."

Someone who had forgotten to breathe lately gave a long, deep suspiration.

Hassell handed the eighth slip to the Director-General.

"Lewis Taine."

The tension broke. Everyone crowded around the three chosen men. For a moment Hassell stood perfectly still; then he turned toward the others. His face showed absolutely no emotion of any kind. Then Professor Maxton clapped him on the shoulder and said something that Dirk could not hear. Hassell's face relaxed and he answered with a wry smile. Dirk distinctly caught the word "Mars"; then, looking quite cheerful, Hassell joined the others in congratulating his friends.

"That'll do!" boomed the Director-General, grinning all over his face. "Come across to my office—I may have a few unopened bottles around the place."

The company trooped next door, only McAndrews excusing himself on the grounds that he had to get hold of the press. For the next quarter of an hour several sedate toasts were drunk in some excellent Australian wines which the Director-General had obviously obtained for this occasion. Then the little party broke up with a general air of relieved satisfaction. Leduc, Richards and Taine were dragged off to face the cameras, while Hassell and Clinton remained for a while in conference with Sir Robert. No one ever knew exactly what he said to them, but they both seemed quite cheerful when they emerged.

When the little ceremony was over, Dirk attached himself to Professor Maxton, who also seemed very pleased with himself and was whistling tunelessly.

"I bet you're glad that's over," said Dirk.

"I certainly am. Now we all know where we stand."

They walked together for a few yards without saying anything. Then Dirk remarked, very innocently: "Have I ever told you about my particular hobby?"

Professor Maxton looked somewhat taken aback. "No; what is it?"

Dirk gave an apologetic cough.

"I'm supposed to be quite a good amateur conjurer."

Professor Maxton stopped his whistling, very abruptly. A profound silence fell. Then Dirk said reassuringly: "There's no need to worry. I'm quite sure that no one else noticed anything—particularly Hassell."

"You," said Professor Maxton firmly, "are a confounded nuisance. I suppose you'll want to put this down in your infernal history?"

Dirk chuckled.

"Perhaps, though I'm not a gossip writer. I noticed that you only palmed Hassell's slip, so presumably the others *were* chosen by chance. Or had you already arranged what names the D.-G. would call out? Were all those blanks genuine, for instance?"

"You are a suspicious blighter! No, the others really were chosen by fair ballot."

"What do you think Hassell will do now?"

"He'll stay for the take-off, and still be home with time to spare."

"And Clinton—how will he take it?"

"He's a phlegmatic individual; it won't worry him.

We're getting the pair of them working right away on the plans for the next trip. That should keep them from fretting and moping."

He turned anxiously to Dirk.

"You'll promise never to say anything about this?"

Dirk gave a grin.

" 'Never' is a heck of a long time. Shall we settle for the year 2000?"

"Always thinking about posterity, aren't you? Very well then—the year 2000 it is. But on one condition!"

"What's that?"

"I'll expect a *de luxe,* autographed copy of your report to read through in my old age!"

6

Dirk was making a tentative draft of his preface when the telephone rang noisily. The fact that he had a telephone at all was somewhat surprising, for many much more important people lacked one and were always coming in to borrow his. But it had fallen out that way during the allocation of offices, and although he expected to lose it at any moment no one had yet arrived to remove the instrument.

"That you, Dirk? Ray Collins here. We've got the screens off the 'Prometheus' so you can see the whole ship at last. And you remember asking me how we serviced the motors?"

"Yes."

"Come along and you can watch. It's worth seeing."

Dirk sighed and put away his notes. One day he would really get started, and then the history would materialize at a terrific rate. He was not at all worried, for he now knew his methods of working. It was no good starting before he had marshaled all the facts, and as yet he had not finished indexing his notes and references.

It was a very cold day, and he wrapped himself

up thoroughly as he walked toward "Oxford Circus." Most of Luna City's traffic converged upon this intersection, and he should be able to get a lift to the launching site. Transport was precious at the base and there was a continual battle between the various departments for the possession of the few available trucks and cars.

He stamped around in the cold for about ten minutes before a jeep loaded with journalists on the same mission came roaring by. It looked somewhat like a traveling optician's shop, since it bristled with cameras, telescopes and binoculars. Nevertheless Dirk managed to find room for himself among the window display.

The jeep swirled into the parking area and everyone clambered out, lugging his equipment. Dirk gave a hand to a very small reporter with a very large telescope and tripod—partly out of good nature but partly because he hoped he'd be able to have a look through it himself.

The two great ships now lay bare of all coverings and screens; for the first time one could fully appreciate their size and proportions. "Beta" might, at a casual glance, have been taken for a conventional airliner of fairly normal design. Dirk, who knew very little about aircraft, would not have given her a second glance had he seen her taking off from his local field.

"Alpha" no longer seemed quite so much like a giant shell. The spaceship's radio and navigational equipment had now been extended, and its lines were completely spoiled by a small forest of masts and outriggers of various kinds. Someone inside must have been operating the controls, for occasionally a mast would retract or extend itself farther.

Dirk followed the crowd around to the rear of the ship. A roughly triangular area had been roped off, so that the "Prometheus" was at one apex and they were at the base. The nearest they could get to the machine's driving units was about a hundred yards. Looking into those gaping nozzles, Dirk felt no particular desire to come any closer.

Cameras and binoculars were being brought into action, and presently Dirk managed to get his look through the telescope. The rocket motors seemed only a few yards away, but he could see nothing except a metal pit full of darkness and mystery. Out of that nozzle would soon be coming hundreds of tons of radioactive gas at fifteen thousand miles an hour. Beyond it, hidden in shadow, were the pile elements that no human being could ever again approach.

Someone was coming toward them through the forbidden area—but keeping very close to the rope barrier. As he approached Dirk saw that it was Dr. Collins. The engineer grinned at him and said: "Thought I'd find you here. We're just waiting for the servicing staff to arrive. That's a nice telescope you've got—can I have a look?"

"It isn't mine," explained Dirk. "It belongs to this gentleman here."

The little journalist would be delighted if the Professor cared to have a look—and still more so if he'd explain what there was to see, anyway.

Collins stared intently for some seconds. Then he straightened up and said: "I'm afraid there's not a lot to see at present—we should have a spotlight shining up the jet to illuminate the interior. But you'll be glad of that telescope in a minute."

He gave a wry little smile.

"It's rather a queer feeling, you know," he said to Dirk, "looking at a machine you've helped build yourself—and which you can never go near again without committing suicide."

While he spoke, an extraordinary vehicle was approaching across the concrete. It was a very large truck, not unlike those which television companies use for outside broadcasts, and it was towing a machine at which Dirk could only stare in baffled amazement. As it went past, he had a confused impression of jointed levers, small electric motors, chain drives and worm-wheels, and other devices he could not identify.

The two vehicles came to a halt just inside the danger area. A door opened in the big truck, and half a dozen men clambered out. They uncoupled the trailer, and began connecting it up to three large armored cables which they unwound from drums at the front of the van.

The strange machine suddenly came to life. It rolled forward on its little balloon tires, as though testing its mobility. The jointed levers began to flex and unflex, giving a weird impression of mechanical life. A moment later it started to roll purposefully toward the "Prometheus," the larger machine following behind it at the same speed.

Collins was grinning hugely at Dirk's amazement and the obvious surprise of the journalists around him.

"That's Tin Lizzie," he said, by way of introduction. "She's not really a true robot, as every movement she makes is controlled directly by the men in the van. It takes a crew of three to run her, and it's one of the most highly skilled jobs in the world."

Lizzie was now within a few yards of "Alpha's" jets, and after some precise foot-work with her bogies she came to a gentle halt. A long, thin arm carrying several obscure pieces of machinery disappeared down that ominous tunnel.

"Remote servicing machinery," explained Collins to his interested audience, "has always been one of the most important side-lines of atomic engineering. It was first developed on a large scale for the Manhattan Project during the War. Since then it's become quite an industry in itself. Lizzie is just one of the more spectacular products. She could almost repair a watch —or at least an alarm clock!"

"Just how does the crew control her?" asked Dirk.

"There's a television camera on that arm, so they can see the work just as if they were watching it directly. All movements are carried out by servo motors controlled through those cables."

No one could see what Lizzie was now doing, and it was a long time before she slowly backed away from the rocket. She was carrying, Dirk saw, a curiously shaped bar about three feet long which she held firmly in her metal claws. The two vehicles withdrew three-quarters of the way to the barrier, and as they approached the journalists hastily retreated from that drab gray object in the robot's claws. Collins, however, stood his ground, so Dirk decided it must be safe to remain.

There was a sudden, raucous buzzing from the engineer's coat-pocket, and Dirk jumped a foot in the air. Collins held up his hand and the robot came to a halt about forty feet away. Its controllers, Dirk guessed, must be watching them through the television eyes.

Collins waved his arms, and the bar slowly rotated in the robot's claws. The buzzing of the radiation alarm ceased abruptly and Dirk breathed again.

"There's usually some sort of beaming effect from an irregular object like that," explained Collins. "We're still in its radiation field, of course, but it's too weak to be dangerous."

He turned toward the telescope, which had been temporarily deserted by its owner.

"This is rather handy," he said. "I didn't intend to do a visual inspection myself, but this is too good a chance to miss—that is, if we can focus at this distance."

"Exactly what are you trying to do?" asked Dirk as his friend racked the eyepiece out to its fullest extent.

"That's one of the reactor elements from the pile," said Collins absently. "We want to check it for activity. H'm—it seems to be standing up to it all right. Like a peep?"

Dirk peered through the telescope. He could see a few square inches of what at first sight appeared to be metal; then he decided that it was some kind of ceramic coating. It was so close that he could distinctly make out the surface texture.

"What would happen," he said, "if you touched it?"

"You'd cetainly get very bad delayed burns, gamma

and neutron. If you stayed near it long enough, you'd die."

Dirk stared in fascinated horror at that innocent gray surface which seemed only a few inches away.

"I suppose," he said, "that the bits in an atomic bomb would look very much like this."

"Just as harmless, anyway," agreed Collins. "But there's no danger of an explosion here. The fissionable material we use is all denatured. If we went to a lot of trouble, we *could* get an explosion—but a very small one."

"What do you mean by that?" asked Dirk suspiciously.

"Oh, just a large bang," said Collins cheerfully. "I couldn't give the figures off-hand, but it would probably be no better than a few hundred tons of dynamite. Nothing to worry about at all!"

7

The senior staff lounge always gave Dirk the impression of a slightly down-at-heel London club. The fact that he had never been in a London club—prosperous or otherwise—did nothing to shake this firm conviction.

Yet at any one time the British contingent in the lounge was likely to be in the minority, and almost every accent in the world could be heard here during the course of the day. It made no difference to the atmosphere of the place, which seemed to emanate from the very English barman and his two assistants. Despite all onslaughts, they had kept the Union Jack flying here in the social center of Luna City. Only once had they yielded any territory, and even then the enemy had been swiftly routed. Six months ago the Americans had imported a brand-new Coca-Cola machine, which for a while had gleamed resplendently against the somber wooden paneling. But not for long: there had been some hasty consultations and much midnight carpentry

in the workshops. One morning when the thirsty cli-
ents arrived, they found that the chromium plating had
disappeared, and that they must now obtain their
drinks from what might have been one of the late Mr.
Chippendale's minor masterpieces. The *status quo* had
been restored, but as to how it had happened the barman confessed complete ignorance.

Dirk always called at least once a day to collect his
mail and read the papers. In the evening the place
usually became rather crowded and he preferred to
stay in his room, but tonight Maxton and Collins had
dragged him out of retirement. The conversation, as
usual, was not very far from the enterprise at hand.

"I think I'll be going to Taine's lecture tomorrow,"
said Dirk. "He's talking about the Moon, isn't he?"

"Yes; I bet he'll be pretty cautious now that he
knows he's going! He might have to eat his words if
he's not careful."

"We've given him a perfectly free hand," explained
Maxton. "He'll probably talk about long-term plans
and the use of the Moon as a refueling base to reach
the planets."

"That should be interesting. Richards and Clinton
will both be talking about engineering, I suppose,
and I've had quite enough of that."

"Thanks!" laughed Collins. "It's nice to know that
our efforts are appreciated!"

"Do you know," said Dirk suddenly, "I've never
even seen the Moon through a big telescope."

"We could fix that up any evening this week—say
after tomorrow. The Moon's only a day old at the moment. There are several telescopes here that would give
you a pretty good view."

"I wonder," said Dirk thoughtfully, "if we're going
to find life—I mean intelligent life—anywhere in the
solar system?"

There was a long pause. Then Maxton said
abruptly: "I don't think so."

"Why not?"

"Look at it this way. It's taken us only ten thousand

years to get away from stone axes to spaceships. That means that interplanetary travel must come pretty early in the development of any culture—that is, if it proceeds along technological lines at all."

"But it needn't," said Dirk. "And if you throw in prehistory, it's taken us a million years to get to spaceships."

"That's still only a thousandth—or less—of the age of the solar system. If there was any civilization on Mars, it probably died before humanity emerged from the jungle. If it still flourished, it would have visited us long ago."

"That's so plausible," replied Dirk, "that I'm sure it isn't true. Moreover, you can find plenty of incidents which make it look as if we *have* been visited in the past, by things or ships that didn't like the look of us and sheered off again."

"Yes, I've read some of those accounts, and they're very interesting too. But I'm a skeptic: if anything ever has visited Earth, which I doubt, I'll be very surprised if it came from the other planets. Space and time are so big that it just doesn't seem probable that we'll have neighbors only across the road."

"That seems a pity," said Dirk. "I think the most exciting thing about astronautics is the possibility it opens up of meeting other types of minds. It won't make the human race seem quite so lonely."

"That's perfectly true; but perhaps it will be just as well if we can spend the next few centuries quietly exploring the solar system by ourselves. At the end of that time we'll have acquired a lot more wisdom—and I *mean* wisdom, not mere knowledge. Perhaps we'll be ready then to make contact with other races. At the moment—well, we're still only forty years from Hitler."

"Then how long do you think we'll have to wait," said Dirk, a little discouraged, "before we have our first contact with another civilization?"

"Who can say? It may be as near in time as the Wright Brothers—or as far away as the building of the pyramids. It may even, of course, happen a week from tomorrow when the 'Promtheus' lands on the Moon. But I'm darned sure it won't."

"Do your really think," asked Dirk, "that we'll ever get to the stars?"

Professor Maxton sat in silence for a moment, thoughtfully blowing clouds of cigarette smoke.

"I think so. Some day," he said.

"How?" persisted Dirk."

"If we can get an atomic drive that's more than fifty per cent efficient, we can reach nearly the velocity of light—perhaps three-quarters of it, at any rate. That means it's about five years' traveling from star to star. A long time, but still possible even for us short-lived creatures. And one day, I hope, we'll live a lot longer than we do today. A *heck* of a lot longer."

Dirk had a sudden vision of the three of them from the point of view of an outside observer. He sometimes had these moments of objectivity, and they were valuable in preserving his sense of proportion. Here they were, two men in the thirties and one in the fifties, sitting in their armchairs around the low table carrying their drinks. They might have been businessmen discussing a deal, or resting after a round of golf. Their background was utterly commonplace; from time to time snatches of everyday conversation drifted across from other groups, and there was a faint "clicking" of table-tennis balls from the room next door.

Yes, they might have been discussing stocks and shares, or the new car, or the latest gossip. But instead, they were wondering how to reach the stars.

"Our present atomic drives," said Collins, "are about one hundredth of one per cent efficient. So it will be quite a while before we think of going to Alpha Centauri."

(*In the background a plaintive voice was saying: "Hey, George, what's happened to my gin and lime?"*)

"Another question," said Dirk. "Is it absolutely certain that we can't travel faster than light?"

"In this universe, yes. It's the limiting velocity for all material objects. A miserable six hundred million miles an hour!"

(*"Three bitters, please, George!"*)

"Still," said Maxton slowly and thoughtfully, "there may even be a way around that."

"What do you mean?" asked Dirk and Collins simultaneously.

"In *our* universe, two points may be light-years apart. But they might be almost touching in a higher space."

(*"Where's the* Times? *No, you ass, not the New York thing!"*)

"I draw the line at the fourth dimension," said Collins with a grin. "That's a bit too fantastic for me. I'm a practical engineer—I hope!"

(*In the table-tennis room next door, it sounded as if an absent-minded victor had just jumped the net to shake hands with his opponent.*)

"At the beginning of this century," Professor Maxton retorted, "practical engineers felt the same way about the theory of relativity. But it caught up with them a generation later." He rested his elbows on the table and stared into the remote distance.

"What," he said slowly, "do you imagine the *next* hundred years will bring?"

8

The big Nissen hut was supposed to be connected to the camp's heating system, but no one would have noticed it. Dirk, who had grown accustomed to life at Luna City, had wisely brought his overcoat with him. He felt sorry for the unfortunate members of the audience who had neglected this elementary precaution. By the end of the lecture, they would have a vivid impression of conditions on the outer planets.

About two hundred people were already seated on the benches, and more were continually arriving, since it was still only five minutes after the time at which the lecture was supposed to start. In the middle of the room a couple of anxious electricians were making last-minute adjustments to an episcope. Half a dozen armchairs had been placed in front of the speaker's dais, and were the targets of many covetous eyes. As clearly as if they had been labeled, they proclaimed to the world: "Reserved for the Director-General."

A door at the back of the hut opened, and Sir Robert Derwent entered, followed by Taine, Professor Maxton, and several others whom Dirk did not recognize. All but Sir Robert sat down in the front row, leaving the center seat empty.

The shuffling and whispering ceased as the Director-General stepped on to the dais. He looked, Dirk thought, like some great impresario about to ring up the curtain. And so, in a sense, he was.

"Mr. Taine," said Sir Robert, "has kindly consented to give us a talk on the objects of our first expedition. As he was one of its planners, and as he will be taking part in it, I'm sure we'll hear his views with great interest. After he's talked about the Moon, I gather that Mr. Taine is going to—er—let his hair down and discuss the plans we have for the rest of the solar system. I believe he has it pretty well organized all the way out to Pluto. Mr. Taine."—(Applause.)

As he climbed on to the platform, Dirk studied the astonomer carefully. He had paid little attention to him until now: indeed, apart from his chance meeting with Hassell he had had few opportunities of studying any of the crew.

Taine was a slightly plump young man who seemed scarcely in the middle twenties, though he was actually just under thirty. Astronautics, thought Dirk, certainly catches them young. No wonder that Richards, at thirty-five, was considered quite an old crock by his colleagues.

When he spoke, Taine's voice was dry and precise and his words carried clearly throughout the hut. He was a good speaker, but had an annoying habit of juggling with pieces of chalk—which he frequently missed.

"I needn't tell you very much about the Moon as a whole," he said, "since you've already read or heard quite enough about it in the past few weeks. But I'll discuss the place where we intend to land, and say what we hope to do when we get there.

"First of all, here's a view of the whole Moon. (Slide One, please.) Since it's full, and the sun is shining vertically on the center of the disc, everything looks flat and uninteresting. The dark area here at the bottom right is the Mare Imbrium, in which we'll be landing.

"Now this is the Moon when she's nine days old—which is how you'll see her from Earth when we arrive. As the sun's shining at an angle, you'll see that the mountains near the center show up very clearly—look at those long shadows they throw.

"Let's go closer and examine the Mare Imbrium in detail. The name, by the way, means 'Sea of Rains,' but of course it isn't a sea and it doesn't rain there or anywhere else on the Moon. The old astrologers called it that in the days before the invention of the telescope.

"You'll see from this close-up that the Mare is a fairly flat plain bounded at the top (that's the south, by the way) by this really magnificent range—the lunar Apennines. To the north we have this smaller range, the Alps. The scale here gives you an idea of the distances: that crater, for example, is about fifty miles across.

"This area is one of the most interesting ones on the Moon, and certainly has the finest scenery, but we can only explore a small region on our first visit. We shall land about here (Next Slide, please), and this is a drawing of the area under the greatest magnification we can use. It's as you'd see it with the naked eye from a distance of two hundred miles away in space.

"The exact spot for the landing will be decided during the approach. We'll be falling slowly for the last hundred miles and should have time to select a suitable area. Since we're coming down vertically on shock absorbers, and holding off against the rockets until the last moment, we need only a few square yards of reasonably horizontal surface. Some pessimist has suggested that we may depend on what turns out to be dry quicksand, but this doesn't seem at all likely.

"We will leave the ship in couples, roped together, while one remains aboard to relay messages back to Earth. Our spacesuits carry air for twelve hours, and will insulate us against the whole range of temperatures encountered on the Moon—that is, from boiling point to a couple of hundred degrees below zero, Fahrenheit. Since we'll be there during the daytime, we won't run into the low temperatures unless we stay in shadow for long periods.

"I can't hope to mention all the work we intend to do during our week on the Moon, so I'll merely touch on some of the highlights.

"First of all, we're taking some compact but very powerful telescopes and hope to get clearer views of the planets than have ever been possible before. This equipment, like much of our stores, will be left behind for future expeditions.

"We are bringing back thousands of geological— I should say 'selenological'—samples for analysis. We're looking for mineral containing hydrogen, since once we can estabish a fuel extraction plant on the Moon, the cost of voyages will be cut to a tenth or even less. More important still, we can start thinking of trips to the other planets.

"We're also taking a good deal of radio gear. As you know, the Moon has enormous possibilities as a relay station and we hope to investigate some of these. In addition we shall be making all sorts of physical measurements which will be of the greatest scientific interest. One of the most important of these is the determination of the Moon's magnetic field in order to test Blackett's theory. And, of course, we hope to get a splendid collection of photographs and films.

"Sir Robert has promised you that I'm going to 'let my hair down.' Well, I don't know about that but you may be interested in what I, personally, think the lines of development will be in the next decade or so.

"First of all, we have to establish a semi-permanent base on the Moon. If we're lucky in our first choice, we may be able to build it where we make our initial landing. Otherwise we'll have to try again.

"Quite extensive plans have been drawn up for such a base. It would be self-contained as far as possible, and would grow its own food supplies under glass. The Moon, with its fourteen days continuous sunlight, should be a horticulturist's paradise!

"As we learn more about the Moon's natural resources, the base will be expanded and developed. We expect mining operations at an early date—but they will be to provide materials for use on the Moon. It will be far too expensive to import any but very rare substances to Earth.

"At the present time, journeys to the Moon are extremely costly and difficult because we have to carry fuel for the return trip. When we can refuel on the Moon, we shall be able to use much smaller and more economical machines. And, as I remarked just now, we'll be able to go to the planets.

"It sounds paradoxical, but it's easier to make the forty-million-mile journey from a lunar base to Mars than it is to cross the quarter of a million miles between Earth and Moon. It takes much longer, of course—about two hundred and fifty days—but it doesn't take more fuel.

"The Moon, thanks to its low gravitational field, is the stepping-stone to the planets—the base for the exploration of the solar system. If everything goes smoothly, we should be making plans for reaching Mars and Venus about ten years from now.

"I don't propose to speculate about Venus, except to say that we'll almost certainly make a radar survey of her before we attempt a landing. It should be possible to get accurate radar maps of the hidden surface, unless her atmosphere is very odd indeed.

"The exploration of Mars will be very much like the exploration of the Moon in some respects. We may not need spacesuits to go around in, but we'll certainly need oxygen equipment. The Martian base will be up against the same problems as the Lunar one, though in a much less acute form. But it will have one disadvantage—it will be a long way from home and will have to rely much more on its own resources. The almost certain presence of some kind of life will also effect the settlement in ways we can't predict. If there *is* intelligence on Mars—which I doubt— then our plans may have to be changed completely; we may not be able to stay there at all. The possibilities as far as Mars is concerned are almost endless; that's why it's such an interesting place.

"Beyond Mars, the scale of the solar system opens out and we cannot do much exploring until we have faster ships. Even our 'Prometheus' could reach the outer planets, but she couldn't get back and the journey would take many years. However, by the end of the century, I believe we may be getting ready to go to Jupiter and, perhaps, Saturn. Very probably these expeditions will start from Mars.

"We cannot of course hope to *land* on those two planets: if they have solid surfaces at all, which is doubtful, they are thousands of miles down beneath an atmosphere we dare not enter. If there is any form of life inside those subarctic infernos, I don't see how we can ever contact it—or how it can ever know anything about us.

"The chief interest on Saturn and Jupiter lies in their systems of moons. Saturn has at least twelve,

Jupiter at least fifteen. What's more, many of them are fair-sized worlds—bigger than our Moon. Titan, Saturn's largest satellite, is half as big as Earth, and it's known to have an atmosphere, though not a breathable one. They are all very cold indeed, but that is not a serious objection now that we can get unlimited quantities of heat from atomic reactions.

"The three outermost planets won't concern us for quite a long time to come—perhaps fifty years or more. We know very little about them at the moment, in any case.

"That's all I'm going to say now. I hope I've made it clear that the journey we're taking next week, though it seems so tremendous by our present standards, is really only the first step. It's exciting and interesting, but we must keep it in its true perspective. The Moon's a small world, and in some ways not a very promising one, but it will lead us eventually to eight other planets, some bigger than the Earth, and more than thirty moons of various sizes. The total area we're opening up for exploration in the next few decades is at least ten times that of the land surface of this planet. That should provide room for everybody.

"Thank you."

Taine stopped abruptly, without any rhetorical flourishes, like a broadcaster caught out by the studio clock. There was dead silence in the hut for perhaps half a minute as his audience came slowly back to earth. Then there was a polite trickle of applause, which slowly grew as more and more of Taine's listeners discovered that they were still standing on the solid ground.

The reporters, stamping their feet and trying to restore their circulations, began to file out into the open. Dirk wondered how many had realized, for the first time, that the Moon was not a goal but a beginning—the first step upon an infinite road. It was a road, he now believed, along which all races must travel in the end, lest they wither and die upon their little, lonely worlds.

For the first time one could now see the "Prometheus" as a whole. "Alpha" had at last been hoisted into position upon "Beta's" broad shoulders, giving her a somewhat ugly, hunch-backed appearance. Even Dirk, to whom all flying machines looked very much alike, could not now have confused the great ship with anything else that had ever ridden the skies.

He followed Collins up the ladder of the movable gantry for his last look at the interior of the spaceship. It was evening and there were few people about. Beyond the warning ropes some photographers were trying to get shots of the machine with the sun going down behind it. The "Prometheus" would make an impressive sight silhouetted against the fading glory of the western sky.

"Alpha's" cabin was as bright and tidy as an operating theater. Yet there were personal touches: here and there articles which obviously belonged to the crew had been stowed away in niches where they were firmly secured with elastic bands. Several pictures and photographs had been pasted against convenient walls, and over the pilot's desk a plastic frame carried a portrait of (So Dirk assumed) Leduc's wife. Charts and mathematical tables had been secured at strategic spots where they could be quickly consulted. Dirk suddenly remembered, for the first time in days, his visit to the training mock-up in England, where he had stood before this same array of instruments in a quiet London suburb. That seemed a lifetime ago, and more than half a world away.

Collins walked over to a tall locker and swung open the door.

"You haven't seen one of these before, have you?" he asked.

The three flaccid spacesuits hanging from their hooks looked like creatures of the deep sea, dredged up from the darkness into the light of day. The thick, flexible covering yielded easily at Dirk's touch, and he felt the presence of reinforcing metal hoops. Transparent helmets like large goldfish bowls were secured in recesses at the side of the locker.

"Just like diving suits, aren't they?" said Collins. "As a matter of fact, 'Alpha' is more like a submarine than anything else—though our design problems are a lot easier, as we haven't such pressures to contend with."

"I'd like to sit in the pilot's position," said Dirk abruptly. "Is it all right?"

"Yes, as long as you don't touch anything."

Collins watched with a slight smile as the other settled himself down in the seat. He knew the impulse, having yielded to it himself more often than once.

When the ship was under power, or standing vertically on the Moon, the seat would have swung forward through a right angle from its present position. What was now the floor beneath Dirk's feet would then be the wall in front of him, and the periscope eyepiece which his boots now had to avoid would be conveniently placed for his use. Because of this rotation—so unfamiliar to the human mind—it was hard to capture the sensations which the ship's pilot would have when he occupied this seat.

Dirk rose and turned to go. He followed Collins in silence to the airlock, but paused for a moment at the thick oval door for a last look around the quiet cabin.

"Good-bye, little ship," he said in his mind. "Good-bye—and good luck!"

It was dark when they stepped out on to the gantry, and the floodlights spilled pools of brilliance upon the concrete below. A cold wind was blowing, and the night blazed with stars of which he would never know the names. Suddenly Collins, standing in the gloom beside him, caught his arm and pointed silently to the horizon.

Almost lost in the faint afterglow of the sunset, the two-day-old sickle of the New Moon was sliding down into the west. Clasped in its arms was the dimly lumi-

nous disk which still awaited the advent of day. Dirk
tried to picture the great mountains and the wrinkled
plains still waiting for the sun to rise upon them, yet
already ablaze with the cold light of the almost full
Earth.

Millions upon millions of times the Earth had
waxed and waned above the silent land, and only
shadows had ever moved upon its face. Since the dawn
of terrestrial life, perhaps a dozen craters had crumbled
and decayed, but it had known no other change than
this. And now at last, after all these ages, its loneliness
was coming to an end.

9

Two days before take-off, Luna City was probably one
of the calmest and least agitated spots on Earth. All
preparations had been completed except the final fueling and some last-minute tests. There was nothing to
do except wait until the Moon moved to its appointed
place.

In the great newspaper offices all over the planet,
sub-editors were busily preparing their headlines, and
writing possible alternative stories which could be
quickly trimmed to fit all but the most stubborn facts.
Perfect strangers in buses and trains were liable to
swap astronomical knowledge at the slightest provoca-
tion. Only a very spectacular murder was likely to receive the attention it normally commanded.

In every continent, long-range radar sets were being
tuned up to follow "Alpha" on its journey into space.
The little radar beacon aboard the spaceship would
enable its position to be checked at every moment of
the voyage.

Fifty feet underground at Princeton University, one
of the world's greatest electronic computers was standing by. Should it be necessary for any reason for the
ship to change its orbit, or to delay its return, a new

trajectory must be calculated through the shifting gravitational fields of Earth and Moon. An army of mathematicians would take months to do this; the Princeton calculator could produce the answer, already printed, in a few hours.

Every radio amateur in the world who could operater on the spaceship's frequency was giving his equipment a last-minute check. There would not be many who could both receive and interpret the hyperfrequency, pulse-modulated signals from the ship, but there would be a few. The watch-dogs of the ether, the Communications Commissioners, were standing by to deal with any unauthorized transmitters which might try to break into the circuit.

On their mountain tops, the astronomers were preparing for their private race—the contest to see who would get the best and clearest photographs of the landing. "Alpha" was far too small to be seen when it reached the Moon—but the flare of the jets as they splashed across the lunar rocks should be visible at least a million miles away.

Meanwhile the three men who held the center of the world's stage gave interviews when they felt like it, slept long hours in their huts, or relaxed violently at table-tennis, which was about the only form of sport that Luna City provided. Leduc, who had a macabre sense of humor, amused himself by telling his friends the useless or insulting things he had left them in his will. Richards behaved as if nothing of the slightest importance had happened, and insisted on making elaborate social engagements for three weeks' time. Taine was seldom seen at all; it transpired later that he was busily writing a mathematical treatise which had very little to do with astronautics. It was, in fact, concerned with the total possible number of games of bridge, and the length of time it would take to play them all.

Very few people indeed knew that the meticulous Taine could, had he wished, have made much more money out of fifty-two pieces of card than he was ever likely to from astronomy. Not that he would do at all badly now, if he came back safely from the Moon. . . .

Sir Robert Derwent lay completely relaxed in his arm-chair, the room in darkness save for the pool of light from the reading lamp He was almost sorry that the two or three days' margin for last-minute hold-ups had not been required. It was still a night and a day and a night again before the take-off—and there was nothing to do but wait.

The Director-General did not like waiting. It gave him time to think, and thought was the enemy of contentment. Now, in the quiet hours of the night, as the greatest moment of his life approached, he was revisiting the past in search of his youth.

The forty years of struggle, of success and heart break, still lay in the future. He was a boy again, at the very beginning of his university career, and the Second World War which had stolen six years of his life was still no more than a threatening cloud on the horizon. He was lying in a Shropshire wood on one of those spring mornings that had never come again, and the book he was reading was the one he still held in his hands. In faded ink upon the fly-leaf were the words, written in a curiously half-formed hand: "Robert A. Derwent. 22 June 1935."

The book was the same—but where, now, was the music of the singing words that once had set his heart on fire? He was too wise and too old; the tricks of alliteration and repetition could not deceive him now, and the emptiness of thought was all too clear. Yet ever and again there would come a faint echo from the past, and for a moment the blood would rush to his cheeks as it had done those forty years ago. Sometimes a single phrase would be enough:

"O Love's lute heard about the lands of Death!"

Sometimes a couplet:

"Until God loosen over land and sea
The thunder of the trumpets of the night."

The Director-General stared into space. He himself was loosening such a thunder as the world had never heard before. Upon the Indian Ocean the sailors would look up from their ships as those roaring motors stormed across the sky; the tea-planters of Ceylon would hear them, now faint and thin, going westward into Africa. The Arabian oilfields would catch the last reverberations as they filtered down from the fringe of space.

Sir Robert turned the pages idly, halting wherever the flying words caught his mind.

"It is not much that a man can save
On the sands of life, in the straits of time,
Who swims in sight of the third great wave,
That never a swimmer shall cross or climb."

What had he saved from Time? Far more, he knew, than most men. Yet he had been almost forty before he had found any aim in life. His love for mathematics had always been with him, but for long it had been a purposeless passion. Even now, it seemed that chance had made him what he was.

"There lived a singer in France of old
By the tideless dolorous midland sea.
In a land of sand and ruin and gold
There shone one woman, and none but she."

The magic failed and faded. His mind went back to the war years, when he had fought in that silent battle of the laboratories. While men were dying on land and sea and air, he had been tracing the paths of electrons through interlocking magnetic fields. Nothing could have been more remotely academic; yet from the work in which he had shared had come the greatest tactical weapon of the war.

It had been a small step from radar to celestial mechanics, from electron orbits to the paths of planets round the sun. The techniques he had applied in the little world of the magnetron could be used again on the cosmic scale. Perhaps he had been lucky; after only ten years of work he had made his reputation through his attack on the three-body problem. Ten years later, somewhat to everyone's surprise—including his own—he had been Astronomer Royal.

> *"The pulse of war and passion of wonder,*
> *The heavens that murmur, the sounds that*
> *shine,*
> *The stars that sing and the loves that thunder,*
> *The music burning at heart like wine. . . ."*

He might have held that post efficiently and with success for the remainder of his life, but the *Zeitgeist* of astronautics had been too strong for him. His mind had told him that the crossing of space was about to come, but how near it was he had not at first recognized. When that knowledge had finally dawned, he had known at last the purpose of his life, and the long years of toil had reaped their harvest.

> *"Ah, had I not taken my life up and given*
> *All that life gives and the years let go,*
> *The wine and honey, the balm and leaven,*
> *The dreams reared high and the hopes*
> *brought low?"*

He flicked the yellowing pages a dozen at a time, until his eyes caught the narrow columns of print for which he had been searching. Here at least the magic lingered; here nothing had altered, and the words still beat against his brain with the old, insistent rhythm. There had been a time when the verses, head to tail in an endless chain, had threaded their way through his mind for hour upon hour until the very words had lost their meaning:

"Then star nor sun shall waken,
Nor any change of light:
Nor sound of waters shaken,
Nor any sound or sight:
Nor wintry leaves nor vernal,
Nor days nor things-diurnal;
Only the sleep eternal
In an eternal night."

The eternal night would come, and too soon for Man's liking. But at least before they guttered and died, he would have known the stars; before it faded like a dream, the Universe would have yielded up its secrets to his mind. Or if not to his, then to the minds that would come after and would finish what he had now begun.

Sir Robert closed the slim volume and place it back upon the shelf. His voyage into the past had ended in the future, and it was time to return.

Beside his bed, the telephone began to call for attention in angry, urgent bursts.

10

No one ever learned a great deal about Jefferson Wilkes, simply because there was very little indeed to know about him. He had been a junior accountant in a Pittsburgh factory for almost thirty years, during which time he had been promoted once. He did his work with a laborious thoroughness that was the despair of his employers. Like millions of his contemporaries, he had practically no understanding of the civilization in which he found himself. Twenty-five years ago he had married, and no one was surprised to discover that his wife had left him in a matter of months.

Not even his friends—though there was no evidence that he had ever possessed any—would have maintained that Jefferson Wilkes was a profound thinker.

Yet there was one matter to which, after his fashion, he had given very serious thought.

The world would never know what had first turned the pathetic little mind of Jefferson Wilkes outward toward the stars. It was more than probable that the motive had been a desire to escape from the drab reality of his everyday life. Whatever the reason, he had studied the writings of those who predicted the conquest of space. And he had decided that, at all costs, it must be stopped.

As far as could be gathered, Jefferson Wilkes believed that the attempt to enter space would bring down upon humanity some stupendous metaphysical doom. There was even evidence that he considered the Moon to be Hell, or at least Purgatory. Any premature arrival by mankind in those infernal regions would obviously have incalculable and—to say the least—unfortunate consequences.

To gain support for his ideas, Jefferson Wilkes did what thousands before him had done. He sought to convert others to his beliefs by forming an organization to which he gave the declamatory title: "The Rockets Must Not Rise!" Since any doctrine, however fantastic, will gain some adherents, Wilkes eventually acquired a few score supporters among the obscurer religious sects that flourish exotically in the western United States. Very swiftly, however, the microscopic movement was rent by schism and counter-schism. At the end of it all, the Founder was left with shattered nerves and depleted finances. If one wishes to draw so fine a distinction, it may be said that he then became insane.

When the "Prometheus" was built, Wilks decided that her departure could only be prevented by his own efforts. A few weeks before the take-off, he liquidated his meager assets and withdrew his remaining money from the bank. He found that he would still need one hundred and fifty-five dollars to take him to Australia.

The disappearance of Jefferson Wilkes surprised and pained his employers, but after a hasty inspection of his books they made no efforts to trace him. One does not call in the police when, after thirty years of faithful service, a member of the staff steals one hundred and fifty-five dollars from a safe containing several thousand.

Wilkes had no difficulty in reaching Luna City, and when he was there no one took any notice of him. Interplanetary's staff probably thought he was one of the hundreds of reporters around the base, while the reporters took him for a member of the staff. He was, in any case, the sort of man who could have walked straight into Buckingham Palace without attracting the slightest attention—and the sentries would have sworn that no one had entered.

What thoughts passed through the narrow gateway of Jefferson Wilkes's mind when he saw the "Prometheus" lying on her launching cradle, no one will ever know. Perhaps until that moment he had not realized the magnitude of the task he had set himself. He could have done great damage with a bomb—but though bombs may be come by in Pittsburgh as in all great cities, the ways of acquiring them are not common knowledge—particularly among respectable accountants.

From the rope barriers, whose purpose he could not fully comprehend, he had watched the stores being loaded and the engineers making their final tests. He had noticed that, when night came, the great ship was left unattended beneath the floodlights, and that even these were switched off in the small hours of the morning.

Would it not be far better, he thought, to let the ship leave Earth but to ensure that it would never return? A damaged ship could be repaired; one that vanished without explanation would be a far more effective deterrent—a warning that might be heeded.

Jefferson Wilkes's mind was innocent of science, but he knew that a spaceship must carry its own air supply, and he knew that air was kept in cylinders. What would be simpler than to empty them so that the loss would not be discovered until too late? He did not wish to harm the crew, and was sincerely sorry that they would come to such an end, but he saw no alternative.

It would be tedious to enumerate the defects in Jefferson Wilkes's brilliant plan. The air supply of the "Prometheus" was not even carried in cylinders, and had Wilkes managed to empty the liquid oxygen tanks he would have had some unpleasantly frigid surprises. The routine instrument check would, in any case, have told the crew exactly what had happened before take-off, and even without an oxygen reserve the air-conditioning plant could have maintained a breathable atmosphere for many hours. There would have been time to enter one of the emergency return orbits which could be quickly computed for just such a calamity.

Last, and far from least, Wilkes had to get aboard the ship. He did not doubt that this could be done, for the gantry was left in position every night, and he had studied it so carefully that he could climb it even in the dark. When the crowd had been surging around the head of the ship, he had mingled with it and had seen no sign of locks on that curious, inward-opening door.

He waited in an empty hangar at the edge of the field until the thin moon had set. It was very cold, and he had not been prepared for this since it was summertime in Pennsylvania. But his mission had made him resolute and when at last the blazing floodlights died he had started to cross that empty sea of concrete toward the black wings spread beneath the stars.

The rope barrier halted him and he ducked under it. A few minutes later his groping hands felt a metal framework in the darkness before him, and he made his way around the base of the gantry. He paused at the foot of the metal steps, listening into the night. The world was utterly silent; on the horizon he could see the glow of such lights as were still burning in Luna City. A few hundred yards away he could just make out the dim silhouettes of buildings and hangars, but they were dark and deserted. He began to climb the steps.

He paused again, listening, at the first platform twenty feet from the ground, and again he was reassured. His electric torch and the tools he thought he might need were heavy in his pockets; he felt a little proud of his foresight and the smoothness with which he had carried out his plan.

That was the last step: he was on the upper platform. He gripped his torch with one hand, and a moment later the walls of the spaceship were smooth and cold beneath his fingers.

Into the building of the "Prometheus" had gone millions of pounds and more millions still of dollars. The scientists who had obtained such sums from governments and great industrial undertakings were not exactly fools. To most men—though not to Jefferson Wilkes—it would have seemed improbable that the fruit of all their labors should be left unguarded and unprotected in the night.

Many years ago the planning staff had foreseen the possibility of sabotage by religious fanatics, and one of Interplanetary's most cherished files contained the threatening letters which these people had been illogical enough to write. All reasonable precautions had therefore been taken—and taken by experts, some of whom had themselves spent years during the War sabotaging Axis or Allied equipment.

Tonight the watchman in the concrete bunker at the edge of the macadam was a law student named Achmet Singh, who was earning a little money during his vacation in a way that suited him very well. He had only to be at his post eight hours a day, and the job gave him ample time for study. When Jefferson Wilkes came to the first rope barrier, Achmet Singh was fast asleep —as, surprisingly enough, he was quite expected to be. But five seconds later, he was wide awake.

Singh punched the alarm cut-off button, and moved swiftly across to the control panel, cursing fluently in three languages and four religions. This was the second time this had happened on his watch: before, a stray dog belonging to one of the staff had set off the alarms. The same thing had probably happened again.

He switched on the image converter, waiting impatiently for the few seconds it took the tubes to warm up. Then he grasped the projector controls and started to survey the ship.

To Achmet Singh, it seemed that a purple searchlight was shining across the concrete toward the launching platform. Through the beam of the searchlight, utterly unconscious of its presence, a man was cautiously feeling his way toward the "Prometheus." It was impossible not to laugh at his movements as he groped blindly along while all around him was bathed with light. Achmet Singh followed him steadily with the beam of the infra-red projector until he came to the gantry. The secondary alarms went into action then, and again Singh switched them off. He would not act, he decided, until he had learned the midnight prowler's motives.

When Jefferson Wilkes paused with some satisfaction on the first platform, Achmet Singh secured an excellent photograph which would be conclusive evidence in any court of law. He waited until Wilkes had reached the airlock itself; then he decided to act.

The blast of light which pinned Wilkes against the walls of the spaceship blinded him as effectively as the darkness through which he had been feeling his way. For a moment the shock was so paralyzing that he could not move. Then a great voice roared at him out of the night.

"What are you doing there? Come down at once!"

Automatically he began to stumble down the steps. He had reached the lower platform before his mind lost its paralysis and he looked desperately around for a means of escape. By shielding his eyes, he could now see a little; the fatal ring of floorlights around the "Prometheus" was only a hundred yards across and beyond it lay darkness and, perhaps, safety.

The voice called again from beyond the pool of light.

"Hurry up! Come this way—we've got you covered!"

The "we" was pure invention on the part of Singh, though it was true that reinforcements in the form of two annoyed and sleepy police sergeants were on the way.

Jefferson Wilkes finished his slow descent, and stood trembling with reaction on the concrete, steadying himself against the gantry. He remained almost motionless for half a minute: then, as Achmet Singh had anticipated, he suddenly bolted around the ship and disappeared. He would be running toward the desert, and could be rounded up easily enough, but it would save time if he could be scared back again. The watchman knocked down another loudspeaker switch.

When that same voice roared at him again out of the darkness ahead, where he had thought to find safety, the terrified little spirit of Jefferson Wilkes finally despaired. In unreasoning fear, like some wild animal, he ran back to the ship and tried to hide himself in its shadow. Yet even now the impulse that had brought him round the world still drove him blindly on, though he was scarcely aware of his motives or his actions. He began to work his way along the base of the ship, always keeping in the shadows.

The great hollow shaft only a few feet above his head seemed to offer a second way into the machine —or, at least, a chance of hiding until he could escape. In ordinary times, he could never have made that climb over the smooth metal walls, but fear and determination gave him strength. Achmet Singh, looking into his television screen a hundred yards away, became suddenly ashen. He began to speak, quickly and urgently, into his microphone.

Jefferson Wilkes did not hear him; he scarcely noticed that the great voice from the night was no longer peremptory, but pleading. It meant nothing to him now; he was conscious only of the dark tunnel ahead.

Holding his torch in one hand, he began to crawl along it.

The walls were made of some gray, rock-like material that was hard yet oddly warm to the touch. It seemed to Wilkes as if he was entering a cave with perfectly circular walls; after a few yards it widened and he could almost walk if he bent double. Around him now was a meaningless mosaic of metal bars and that strange gray rock—the most refractory of all ceramics—over which he had been crawling.

He could go no farther; the cave had suddenly divided into a series of branching passages too small for him to enter. Shining his torch along them he could see that the walls were pierced with jets and nozzles. He might have done some damage here, but they were all beyond his reach.

Jefferson Wilkes slumped down on the hard, unyielding floor. The torch fell from his nerveless fingers and the darkness enfolded him again. He was too exhausted for disappointment or regret. He did not notice, nor could he have understood, the faint unwavering glow that was burning in the walls around him.

A long time later, some noise in the external world drew his mind back from wherever it had fled. He sat up and stared around him, not knowing where he was or how he had come here. Far away he could see a faint circle of light, the mouth of this mysterious cavern. Beyond that opening were voices and the sounds of machines moving to and fro. He knew that they were hostile and that he must remain here where they could not find him.

It was not to be. A brilliant light passed like a rising sun across the mouth of his cave, then returned to shine full upon him. It was moving down the tunnel, and behind it was something strange and huge which his mind could not grasp.

He screamed in terror as those metal claws came full into the light and reached forward to grasp him.

Then he was being dragged helplessly out into the open where his unknown enemies were waiting.

There was a confusion of light and noises all around him. A great machine that seemed to be alive was holding him in its metal arms and rolling away from a tremendous winged shape that should have aroused memories, but did not. Then he was lowered to the ground in a circle of waiting men.

He wondered why they did not come near, why they kept so far away and looked at him so strangely. He did not resist when long poles carrying shining instruments were waved around him as if exploring his body. Nothing mattered now; he felt only a dull sickness and an overwhelming desire for sleep.

Suddenly a wave of nausea swept over him and he crumpled to the ground. Impulsively, the men standing in that wide circle moved a pace toward him— and then drew back.

The twisted, infinitely pathetic figure lay like a broken doll beneath the glaring lights. There was no sound or movement anywhere; in the background, the great wings of the "Prometheus" brooded above their pools of shadow. Then the robot glided forward, trailing its armored cables across the concrete. Very gently, the metal arms reached down and the strange hands unfolded.

Jefferson Wilkes had reached the end of his journey.

11

Dirk hoped that the crew had spent a better night than he had. He was still sleepy and confused, but he had a distinct impression of being awakened more than once by the sounds of cars driven recklessly through the night. Perhaps there had been a fire somewhere, but he had heard no alarm.

He was shaving when McAndrews came into his

room, obviously bursting with news. The Director
of Public Relations looked as if he had been up half
the night, which indeed was very nearly the case.

"Have you heard the news?" he said breathlessly.

"*What* news?" asked Dirk, switching off his shaver
with some annoyance.

"There's been an attempt to sabotage the ship."

"What!"

"It happened about one o'clock this morning. The
detectors spotted a man trying to get aboard 'Alpha.'
When the watchman challenged him the damn fool
tried to hide himself—in 'Beta's' exhaust!"

It was some seconds before the full meaning of
the words dawned. Then Dirk remembered what
Collins had told him when he had looked through the
telescope into that deadly pit.

"What happened to him?" he said thickly.

"They called to him through loudspeakers, but he
took no notice. So they had to get him out with the
servicing robot. He was still alive, but too hot to go
near. He died a couple of minutes later. The doctors
say he probably never knew what had happened to
him—you don't when you get a dose like that."

Feeling a little sick, Dirk slumped down on his
bed.

"Did he do any damage?" he asked at length.

"We don't think so. He never got into the ship,
and there was nothing he could do to the jet. They
were afraid he might have left a bomb, but luckily
he hadn't."

"He must have been crazy! Any idea who he was?"

"Probably a religious maniac of some kind. We get
a lot of them after us. The police are trying to trace
him from the contents of his pockets."

There was a gloomy pause before Dirk spoke
again.

"Not a very good send-off for the 'Prometheus,' is
it?"

McAndrews shrugged his shoulders, somewhat
callously.

"I don't think anyone round here's likely to be superstitious! Are you coming out to watch the fueling? It's scheduled for two o'clock. I'll give you a lift down in the car."

Dirk was not enthusiastic.

"Thanks all the same," he said, "but I've got rather a lot to do. And anyway, there won't be much to see, will there? I mean, pumping a few hundred tons of fuel isn't going to be very exciting. I suppose it *could* be—but in that event I'd rather not be there!"

McAndrews seemed slightly annoyed, but Dirk couldn't help that. At the moment he felt singularly little desire to go near the "Prometheus" again. It was an irrational feeling, of course; for why should one blame the great ship if it protected itself against its enemies?

Throughout the day Dirk could hear the roar of helicopters arriving in a continual stream from the great Australian cities, while from time to time a transcontinental jet would come whistling down into the airport. Where these early arrivals expected to spend the night he could not imagine. It was none too warm in the centrally heated huts, and the news reporters unlucky enough to be under canvas had told terrible stories of hardship, many of which were very nearly true.

Late in the afternoon he met Collins and Maxton in the lounge and heard that the fueling had been carried out with no difficulty. As Collins said: "We have now only to light the blue touch-paper and retire."

"By the way," remarked Maxton, "didn't you say the other night that you'd never seen the Moon through a telescope? We're going over to the Observatory in a minute. Why not come along?"

"I'd love to—but don't say that *you've* never looked at her, either!"

Maxton grinned.

"That would be a 'very poor show,' as Ray would put it. I happen to know my way around the Moon quite well, but I doubt if more than half the people in Interplanetary have ever used a telescope. The D.-G.'s the best example of that. He spent ten years on astronomical research before he ever went near an observatory."

"Don't say I told you," said Collins with great seriousness, "but I've found that astronomers are divided into two species. The first is purely nocturnal and spends its working hours taking photos of objects so far away that they probably don't exist any more. They're not interested in the solar system, which they consider a very odd and almost inexcusable accident. During the daytime they may be found sleeping under large stones and in warm, dry places.

"Members of the second species work more normal hours and inhabit offices full of calculating machines and lady computors. This hinders them a lot; nevertheless they manage to produce reams of mathematics about the—probably non-existent—objects photographed by their colleagues, with whom they communicate through little notes left with the nightwatchman.

"Both species have one thing in common. They are never known, except in moments of extreme mental aberration, actually to *look* through their telescopes. Still, they do get some very pretty photographs."

"I think," laughed Professor Maxton, "that the nocturnal species should be emerging any moment now. Let's go."

The "Observatory" at Luna City had been erected largely for the amusement of the technical staff, which included far more amateur astronomers than professionals. It consisted of a group of wooden huts which had been drastically modified to hold about a dozen instruments of all sizes from three to twelve inches' aperture. A twenty-inch reflector was now under construction, but would not be completed for some weeks.

The visitors had, it seemed, already discovered

the Observatory and were making full use of it. Some scores of people were lining up hopefully in front of the various buildings, while the thwarted owners of the telescopes were giving them two-minute peeks accompanied by impromptu lectures. They had not bargained for this when they had gone out to have a look at the four-day-old Moon, and they had now given up all hope of having a view themselves.

"It's a pity they can't charge a pound a head," said Collins thoughtfully as he looked at the queue.

"Perhaps they are," answered Professor Maxton. "We might at least put up a collecting box for impecunious atomic engineers."

The dome of the twelve-inch reflector—the only instrument which was not privately owned and which actually belonged to Interplanetary—was closed and the building was locked. Professor Maxton drew out a bunch of master keys and tried them one by one until the door opened. The nearest in line immediately broke ranks and started to pour toward them.

"Sorry," shouted the Professor, as he slammed the door behind them, "it's out of order!"

"You mean it *will* be out of order," said Collins darkly. "Do you know how to use one of these things?"

"We should be able to figure it out," answered Maxton, with just a shade of uncertainty in his voice.

Dirk's very high opinion of the two scientists began to fall abruptly.

"Do you mean to tell me," he said, "that you're going to risk using an instrument as complicated and expensive as this without knowing anything about it? Why, it would be like someone who didn't know how to drive getting into an automobile and trying to start it!"

"Goodness, gracious," protested Collins, though with a slight twinkle in his eye. "You don't think *this* thing is complicated, do you? Compare it with a bicycle, if you like—but not a car!"

"Very well," retorted Dirk, "just try and ride a bicycle without any practice beforehand!"

Collins merely laughed and continued his examination of the controls. For some time he and the Professor exchanged technical conversation which no longer impressed Dirk, since he could see that they knew very little more about the telescope than he did himself.

After some experimenting, the instrument was swung round to the Moon, now fairly low in the southwest. For a long time, it seemed to Dirk, he waited patiently in the background while the two engineers looked to their full. Finally he got fed up.

"You *did* invite me, you know," he remonstrated. "Or have you forgotten?"

"Sorry," apologized Collins, giving up his position with obvious reluctance. "Have a look now—focus up with this knob."

At first Dirk could see only a blinding whiteness with darker patches here and there. He slowly turned the focusing knob, and suddenly the picture became clear and sharp, like some brilliant etching.

He could see a good half of the crescent, the tips of the horns being out of the field. The edge of the Moon was a perfect arc of a circle, without any sign of unevenness. But the line dividing night and day was ragged, and broken in many places by mountains and uplands which threw long shadows across the plains below. There were few of the great craters he had expected to see, and he guessed that most of them must lie in the part of the disk that was still unlit.

He focused his attention upon a great oval plain bordered with mountains, which reminded him irresistibly of a dried-up ocean bed. It was, he supposed, one of the Moon's so-called seas, but it was easy to tell that there was no water anywhere in that calm, still landscape spread out beneath him. Every detail was sharp and brilliant, save when a ripple like a heat-haze made the whole picture tremble for a moment. The Moon was sinking into the horizon mists, and the image was being disturbed by its slanting, thousand-mile passage through the Earth's atmosphere.

At one point just inside the darkened area of the disk a group of brilliant lights shone like beacon fires blazing in the lunar night. They puzzled Dirk for a moment, until he realized that he was looking upon great mountain peaks which had caught the sun hours before the dawning light had struck into the lowlands around their bases.

He understood now why men had spent their lives watching the shadows come and go across the face of that strange world which seemed so near yet which, until his generation, had been the symbol of all that could never be attained. He realized that in a lifetime one could not exhaust its wonders; always there would be something fresh to see as the eye grew more skilled in tracing out that wealth of almost infinite detail.

Something was blocking his view and he looked up in annoyance. The Moon was descending below the level of the dome; he could lower the telescope no farther. Someone switched on the lights again and he saw that Collins and Maxton were grinning at him.

"I hope you've seen all you want to," said the Professor. "We had ten minutes apiece—*you* have been there for twenty-five and I'm darned glad the Moon set when it did!"

12

"Tomorrow we launch the 'Prometheus.' I say 'we,' because I find it no longer possible to stand aside and play the part of a disinterested spectator. No one on Earth can do that; the events of the next few hours will shape the lives of all men who will ever be born, down to the end of time.

"Someone once pictured humanity as a race of islanders who have not yet learned the art of making ships. Out across the ocean we can see other islands about which we have wondered and speculated since the beginning of history. Now, after a million years, we have made our first primitive canoe; tomorrow we will watch it sail through the coral reef and vanish over the horizon.

"This evening I saw, for the first time in my life, the Moon's glittering mountains and great dusky plains. The country over which Leduc and his companions will be walking in less than a week was still invisible, waiting for the sunrise which will not come for another three of our days. Yet its night must be brilliant beyond imagination, for the Earth will be more than half-full in its sky.

"I wonder how Leduc, Richards and Taine are spending their last night on Earth? They will, of course, have put all their affairs in order, and there'll be nothing left for them to do. Are they relaxing, listening to music, reading—or just sleeping?"

James Richards was doing none of these things. He was seated in the lounge with his friends, drinking very slowly and carefully, while he regaled them with entertaining stories of the tests he had been given by crazy psychologists trying to decide if he was normal, and if so, what could be done about it. The psychologists he was libeling formed the largest—and most appreciative—part of his audience. They let him talk until midnight; then they put him to bed. It took six of them to do it.

Pierre Leduc had spent the evening out at the ship, watching some fuel evaporation tests that were being carried out on "Alpha." There was very little point in his being present, but although gentle hints had been dropped from time to time, no one could get rid of him. Just before midnight the Director-General arrived, exploded goodnaturedly and sent him back in his own car with strict orders to get some sleep. Whereupon Leduc spent the next two hours in bed reading *La Comédie Humaine.*

Only Lewis Taine—the precise, unemotional Taine —had used his last night on Earth in ways that might have been expected. He had sat for hours at his desk preparing drafts and destroying them one by one. Late in the evening he had finished; in careful long-hand he transcribed the letter which had cost him so much thought. Then he sealed it and attached a formal little note:

DEAR PROFESSOR MAXTON,
    If I do not return, I should be obliged if you would arrange for this letter to be delivered.
Sincerely,
L. TAINE.

Letter and note he placed in a large envelope which he addressed to Maxton. Then he picked up the bulky file of alternative flight orbits and began to make pencil notes in the margins.

He was himself again.

13

The message which Sir Robert had been expecting arrived soon after dawn by one of the high-speed mailplanes which, later in the day, would be carrying the films of the launching back to Europe. It was a brief official minute, signed only with a pair of initials which the whole world would have recognized even without the help of the words: "10, Downing Street" which ran along the head of the paper. Yet it was not entirely a formal document, for beneath the initials the same hand had written: "Good luck!"

When Professor Maxton arrived a few minutes later, Sir Robert handed him the paper without a word. The American read it slowly and gave a sigh of relief.

"Well, Bob," he said, "we've done our share. It's up to the politicians now—but we'll keep pushing them from behind."

"It's not been as difficult as I feared; the statesmen have learned to pay attention to us since Hiroshima."

"And when will the plan come up before the General Assembly?"

"In about a month, when the British and American governments will formally propose that 'all planets or celestial bodies unoccupied or unclaimed by non-human forms of life, etc. etc., be deemed international areas freely accessible to all peoples, and that no sovereign state be permitted to claim any such astronomical bodies for its exclusive occupation or development . . .' and so on."

"And what about the proposed Interplanetary Commission?"

"That will have to be discussed later. At the moment the important thing is to get agreement on the first stages. Now that our governments have formally adopted the plan—it will be on the radio by the afternoon—we can start lobbying like hell. You're best at this sort of thing—can you write a little speech on the lines of our first Manifesto—one that Leduc can broadcast from the Moon? Emphasize the astronomical viewpoint, and the stupidity of even attempting to carry nationalism into space. Think you can do it before take-off? Not that it matters if you can't, except that it may leak out too soon if we have to radio the script."

"O.K.—I'll get the rough draft checked over by the political experts, and then leave you to put in the adjectives as usual. But I don't think it will need any purple passages this time. As the first message to come from the Moon, it will have quite enough psychological punch by itself!"

Never before had any part of the Australian desert known such a population density. Special trains from Adelaide and Perth had been arriving throughout the night, and thousands of cars and private aircraft were parked on either side of the launching track. Jeeps were continually patrolling up and down the kilometer-wide safety zones, shooing away too inquisitive visitors. No one at all was allowed past the five-kilometer mark, and at this point the canopy of circling aircrafts also came to an abrupt end.

The "Prometheus" lay glittering in the low sunlight, throwing a fantastic shadow far across the desert. Until now she had seemed only a thing of metal, but at last she was alive and waiting to fulfill the dreams of her creators. The crew was already aboard when Dirk and his companions arrived. There had been a little ceremony for the benefit of the newsreels and television cameras, but no formal speeches. These could come, if they were needed, in three weeks' time.

In quiet, conversational tones the loud-speakers along the track were saying: "Instrument check completed: launching generators running at half speed: one hour to go."

The words came rolling back across the desert, muffled by distance, from the further speakers: "One hour to go—hour to go—go—go—go . . ." until they had died away into the northwest.

"I think we'd better get into position," said Professor Maxton. "It's going to take us some time to drive through this crowd. Take a good look at 'Alpha'—it's the last opportunity you'll have."

The announcer was speaking again, but this time his words were not intended for them. Dirk realized that he was overhearing part of a world-wide sequence of instructions.

"All sounding stations should be ready to fire. Sumatra, India, Iran—let us have your readings within the next fifteen minutes."

Many miles away in the desert, something went screaming up into the sky, leaving behind it a pure white vapor trail that might have been drawn with a ruler. While Dirk watched, the long milky column began to writhe and twist as the winds of the stratosphere dispersed it.

"Met rocket," said Collins, answering his unspoken question. "We've got a chain of them along the flight path, so we'll know pressures and temperatures all the way up to the top of the atmosphere. Just before the take-off, the pilot of 'Beta' will be warned if there's anything unusual ahead of him. That's one worry that Leduc won't have. There's no weather out in space!"

Across Asia, the slim rockets with their fifty kilograms of instruments were climbing through the stratosphere on their way to space. Their fuel had been exhausted in the first few seconds of flight, but their speed was great enough to carry them a hundred kilometers from the Earth. As they rose—some in sunlight, others still in darkness—they sent back to the ground a continual stream of radio impulses, which would be caught and translated and passed on to Australia. Presently they would fall back to Earth, their parachutes would blossom, and most of them would be found and used again. Others, not so fortunate, would fall into the sea or, perhaps, end their days as tribal gods in the jungles of Borneo.

The three-mile drive along the crowded and very primitive road took them nearly twenty minutes, and more than once Professor Maxton had to make a detour into the no-man's-land which he himself had put out of bounds. The concentration of cars and spectators was greatest when they came to the five kilometer mark—and ended abruptly at a barrier of red-painted poles.

A small platform had been erected here from old packing cases, and this improvised stand was already occupied by Sir Robert Derwent and several of his staff. Also present, Dirk noticed with interest, were Hassell and Clinton. He wondered what thoughts were passing through their minds.

From time to time the Director-General made comments into a microphone, and there were one or two portable transmitters around. Dirk, who had vaguely expected to see batteries of instruments, was a little disappointed. He realized that all the technical operations were being carried out elsewhere, and this was merely an observation post.

"Twenty-five minutes to go," said the loud-speakers. "Launching generators will now run up to full operating speed. All radar-tracking stations and observations in the main network should be standing by."

From the low platform, almost the whole of the launching track could be seen. To the right were the massed crowds and beyond them the low buildings of the airport. The "Prometheus" was clearly visible on the horizon, and from time to time the sunlight caught her sides so that they glittered like mirrors.

"Fifteen minutes to go."

Leduc and his companions would be lying in those curious seats, waiting for them to tilt under the first surge of acceleration. Yet it was strange to think that they would have nothing to do for almost an hour, when the separation of the ships would take place high above the Earth. All the initial responsibility lay upon the pilot of "Beta," who would get very little credit for his share in the proceedings—though in any case he was merely repeating what he had done a dozen times before.

"Ten minutes to go. All aircraft are reminded of their safety instructions."

The minutes were ticking past: an age was dying and a new one was being born. And suddenly the impersonal voice from the loud-speakers recalled to Dirk that morning, thirty-three years ago, when another group of scientists had stood waiting in another desert, preparing to unleash the energies that power the suns.

"Five minutes to go. All heavy electrical loads must be shed. Domestic circuits will be cut immediately."

A great silence had come over the crowd; all eyes were fixed upon those shining wings along the skyline.

Somewhere close at hand a child, frightened by the stillness, began to cry.

"One minute to go. Warning rockets away."

There was a great "Swoosh!" from the empty desert over on the left, and a ragged line of crimson flares began to drift slowly down the sky. Some helicopters which had been edging forward minute by minute went hastily into reverse.

"Automatic take-off controller now in operation. Synchronized timing signal—*Now!*"

There was a "click" as the circuit was changed, and the faint rushing of long-distance static came from the speakers. Then there boomed over the desert a sound which, through its very familiarity, could not have been more unexpected.

In Westminster, half way round the world, Big Ben was preparing to strike the hour.

Dirk glanced at Professor Maxton, and saw that he too was completely taken aback. But there was a faint smile on the Director-General's lips, and Dirk remembered that for a half a century Englishmen all over the world had waited beside their radios for that sound from the land which they might never see again. He had a sudden vision of other exiles, in the near or far future, listening upon strange planets to those same bells ringing out across the deeps of space.

A booming silence seemed to fill the desert as the chimes of the last quarter died away, echoing in the distance from one loud-speaker to the next. Then the first stroke of the hour thundered over the desert, and over the waiting world. The speaker circuit was suddenly cut.

Yet nothing had changed: the "Promethus" still lay brooding on the horizon like a great metal moth. Then Dirk saw that the space between her wings and the skyline was a little less than it had been, and a moment later he could tell quite clearly that the ship was expanding as it moved toward him. Faster and faster, in an absolute and uncanny silence, the "Prometheus" came racing down the track. It seemed only a moment before it was abreast of him, and for the very last time he could see "Alpha," smooth and pointed and glittering upon its back. As the ship rushed past to the left out into the empty desert, he could just hear the "swish!" of the air split by its passage. Even that was very faint, and the electric catapult made no sound at all. Then the "Prometheus" was shrinking silently into the distance.

Seconds later, that silence was shattered by a roar as of a thousand waterfalls plunging down the face of mile-high cliffs. The sky seemed to shake and tremble around them; the "Prometheus" itself had vanished from sight behind a cloud of whirling dust. In the heart of that cloud something was burning with an intolerable brilliance that the eye could not have borne for a moment without the intervening haze.

The dust cloud thinned, and the thunder of the jets was softened by distance. Then Dirk could see that the fragment of sun he had been watching through half-shut eyes no longer followed the surface of the Earth, but was lifting, steadily and strongly, up from the horizon. The "Prometheus" was free from her launching cradle, was climbing on the world-wide circuit that would lead her into space.

The fierce white flare dwindled and shrank to nothingness against the empty sky. For a while the mutter of the departing jets rumbled around the heavens until it too was lost, drowned by the noise of circling aircraft.

Dirk scarcely noticed the shouting of the crowds as life returned to the desert behind him. Once again there had come into his mind the picture he was never wholly to forget—that image of the lonely island lost in a boundless and untraveled sea.

Boundless it was, infinite it might be—but it was untraveled no longer. Beyond the lagoon, past the friendly shelter of the coral reef, the first frail ship was sailing into the unknown perils and wonders of the open sea.

Epilogue

Dirk Alexson, sometime Professor of Social History at the University of Chicago, opened the bulky package on his desk with fingers that trembled slightly. For some minutes he struggled with the elaborate wrappings; then the book lay before him, clean and bright as it had left the printers three days ago.

He looked at it silently for a few minutes, running his fingers over the binding. His eyes strayed to the shelf where its five companions rested. They had waited years, most of them, to be joined by this last volume.

Professor Alexson rose to his feet and walked over to the bookshelf, carrying the new arrival with him. A careful observer might have noticed something very odd about his walk: it had a curious springiness that one would not have expected from a man who was nearing sixty. He placed the book beside its five companions, and stood for a long time, completely motionless, staring at the little row of volumes.

The binding and lettering were well matched—he had been very particular about that—and the set was pleasing to the eye. Into those books had gone the greater part of his working life, and now that the task was ended he was well content. Yet it brought a great emptiness of spirit to realize that his work was done.

He took down the sixth volume again and walked back to his desk. He had not the heart to begin at once the search for the misprints, the infelicities which he knew must exist. In any case, they would be brought to his notice soon enough.

The binding protested stiffly as he opened the volume and glanced down the chapter headings, wincing slightly as he came to "Errata—Vols: I-V." Yet he had made few avoidable mistakes—and above all, he had made no enemies. At times in the last decade that had been none too easy. Some of the hundreds of men whose names were in the final index had not been flattered by his words, but no one had ever accused him of undue partiality. He did not believe that anyone could have guessed which of the men in the long and intricate story had been his personal friends.

He turned to the frontispiece—and his mind went back through more than twenty years. There lay the "Prometheus," waiting for the moment of her destiny. Somewhere in that crowd away to the left he himself was standing, a young man with his life's work still before him. And a young man, though he did not know it then, under sentence of death.

Professor Alexson walked over to the window of his study and stared out into the night. The view, as yet, was little obstructed by buildings, and he hoped it would remain that way, so that he could always watch the slow sunrise on the mountains fifteen miles beyond the city.

It was midnight, but the steady white radiance spilling down those tremendous slopes made the scene almost as bright as day. Above the mountains, the stars were shining with that unwavering light that still seemed strange to him. And higher still . . .

Professor Alexson threw back his head and stared through half-closed eyelids at the blinding white world on which he could never walk again. It was very brilliant tonight, for almost all the northern hemisphere was wreathed in dazzling clouds. Only Africa and the Mediterranean regions were unobscured. He remembered that it was winter beneath those clouds; though they looked so beautiful and so brilliant across a quarter of a million miles of space, they would seem a dull and somber gray to the sunless lands they covered.

Winter, summer, autumn, spring—they meant nothing here. He had taken leave of them all when he made his bargain. It was a hard bargain, but a fair one. He had parted from waves and clouds, from winds and rainbows, from the blue skies and the long twilight of summer evenings. In exchange, he had received an indefinite stay of execution.

He remembered, across the years, those endless arguments with Maxton, Collins and the rest about the value of space flight to the human race. Some of their predictions had come true, others had not—but as far as he was concerned, they had proved their case up to the hilt. Matthews had been speaking the truth when he said, long ago, that the greatest benefits which the crossing of space would bring were those which could never have been guessed beforehand.

More than a decade ago the heart specialists had given him three years to live, but the great medical discoveries made at the lunar base had come just in time to save him. Under a sixth of a gravity, where a man weighed less than thirty pounds, a heart which would have failed on Earth could still beat strongly for years. There was even a possibility—almost terrifying in its social implications—that the span of human life might be greater on the Moon than upon the Earth.

Far sooner than anyone had dared to hope, astronautics had paid its greatest and most unexpected dividend. Here within the curve of the Apennines, in the first of all cities ever to be built outside the Earth, five thousand exiles were living useful and happy lives, safe from the deadly gravity of their own world. In time they would rebuild all that they had left behind them; even now the avenue of cedars along Main Street was a brave symbol of the beauty that would be born in the years to come. Professor Alexson hoped he would live to see the building of the Park when the second and much larger Dome was constructed three miles away to the north.

All over the Moon, life was stirring again. It had flickered once, and died, a thousand million years ago; this time it would not fail, for it was part of a rising flood that in a few centuries would have surged to the outermost planets.

Professor Alexson ran his fingers, as he had so often done before, over the piece of Martian sandstone that Victor Hassell had given him years ago. One day, if he wished, he might go to that strange little world; there would soon be ships that could make the crossing in three weeks when the planet was at its nearest. He had changed worlds once; he might do so a second time if he ever became obsessed by the sight of the unattainable Earth.

Beneath its turban of cloud, Earth was taking leave of the twentieth century. In the shining cities, as midnight moved around the world, the crowds would be waiting for the first stroke of the hour which would sunder them forever from the old year and the old century.

Such a hundred years had never been before, and could scarcely come again. One by one the dams had burst, the last frontiers of the mind had been swept away. When the century dawned, Man had been preparing for the conquest of the air; when it died, he was gathering his strength upon Mars for the leap to the outer planets. Only Venus still held him at bay, for no ship had yet been built which could descend through the convection gales raging perpetually between the sunlit hemisphere and the darkness of the Night Side. From only five hundred miles away, the radar screens had shown the pattern of continents and seas beneath those racing clouds—and Venus, not Mars, had become the great enigma of the solar system.

As he saluted the dying century, Professor Alexson felt no regrets: the future was too full of wonder and promise. Once more the proud ships were sailing for unknown lands, bearing the seeds of new civilization which in the ages to come would surpass the old. The rush to the new worlds would destroy the suffocating restraints which had poisoned almost half the century. The barriers had been broken, and men could turn their energies outward to the stars instead of striving among themselves.

Out of the fears and miseries of the Second Dark Age, drawing free—oh, might it be forever!—from the shadows of Belsen and Hiroshima, the world was moving toward its most splendid sunrise. After five hundred years, the Renaissance had come again. The dawn that would burst above the Apennines at the end of the long lunar night would be no more brilliant than the age that had now been born.